DEMON
HUNTERS
TRINITY

DEMON HUNTERS
TRINITY

OLIVIA CHASE

LITTLE, BROWN BOOKS FOR YOUNG READERS
www.lbkids.co.uk

LITTLE, BROWN BOOKS FOR YOUNG READERS

First published in Great Britain in 2016 by Hodder and Stoughton

1 3 5 7 9 10 8 6 4 2

Copyright © Hodder & Stoughton Limited
(on behalf of its imprint Little, Brown Books for Young Readers,
part of Hachette Children's Group) 2016

A CIP catalogue record for this book
is available from the British Library.

ISBN 978-0-349-00227-9

Printed and bound in Great Britain by
Clays Ltd, St Ives plc

The paper and board used in this book are made
from wood from responsible sources.

MIX
Paper from
responsible sources
FSC® C104740

Little, Brown Books for Young Readers
An imprint of
Hachette Children's Group
Part of Hodder and Stoughton
Carmelite House
50 Victoria Embankment
London EC4Y 0DZ

An Hachette UK Company
www.hachette.co.uk

www.hachettechildrens.co.uk

With special thanks to Rosie Best

For Jessie

PROLOGUE

1650, the Mercat Cross, Edinburgh

Thin, freezing sheets of rain broke against the turrets of the Castle and sliced down Lawnmarket towards the High Street. Wave after wave came down from the dark clouds, battering against our cloaks and dancing a ceilidh across the wooden platform at the base of the tall stone pillar. But even the rain seemed to flinch away as it bore down on the crowd that had gathered to see the beheading at the Mercat Cross.

The air around the crowd roiled and bubbled with the heat of their excitement and anger. I saw peasants in thin woollen shawls, traders with their goods wrapped up in tight leather rolls, even a few nobles, feathered hats suffering under the onslaught of the rain.

A crowd will always come out for a killing. Especially for a witch.

I shivered and glanced at Fionna. She was staring up at the platform with tears in her eyes. I saw her grip tighten on the curved sword at her belt.

1

'Courage, Fi,' I whispered.

'I have courage,' she said. The tears spilled over her cheeks and mingled with the rain and vanished. 'Let him come.'

On the platform the Maiden gleamed blackly, flanked by torches. Its construction was simple: a tall triangle of black wood, with a crossbar about four feet from the ground, and, hanging above, a wicked blade. It dripped rain in a ghostly echo of the blood it had spilled down the years. The blood of traitors, Catholics . . . and witches. Women whose only crime was to believe their abusers' superstitious nonsense. The devil was certainly to be found here, but he wasn't the one with his head on the block. He was the one holding the rope.

Gasps rose from the crowd, and then angry jeers and cries full of bloodlust. My hand went to the hilt of my dagger and my blood ran as cold as the sheeting rain. Slowly, a man's head rose up above the rest as he ascended the stairs to the platform.

A wide black hat, greasy grey locks of hair that blew around his sunken cheeks. A pointed grey beard. Thin lips twisted in an expression of snarling triumph.

John Kincaid, the Witch Pricker.

Fionna took an instinctive step forward. I linked my arm in hers, holding her back. We would have our revenge, but it wasn't time yet. We had planned our distraction too carefully to waste it.

Kincaid was dragging a woman behind him. He had her by the hair, a tangle of brown like a handful of thorn twigs. She staggered after him, arms and legs weak and trembling and bloodied. Her clothes hung loose and ragged from her frame, so the pinpricks could be plainly seen. They were scattered across her skin, crusted and weeping. They trailed across her arms, her chest, up her throat and over her cheeks.

I barely even recognised her. This ruined pile of rags and scabs.

Elspeth.

Her rapier hung at my side, but I knew it would be a long time before she could swing it again. Kincaid threw her to the floor and raised his hands to the crowd. They screamed their approval. Behind him Elspeth's twisted hands shot out to break her fall and as they hit the wooden boards she moaned aloud.

Kincaid raised his voice above the bloodlust of the crowd, reciting the lore of the Witch Pricker: '*If a woman hath an area where a pinprick causeth no pain, that woman be a witch and shall be put to death!*'

Or, for anyone whose mind wasn't rotten with superstition and terror: *If you torture someone for days on end, burn the soles of their feet and prick them all over with needles and bobbins and knives, they will confess to anything.*

'This creature is a proven witch,' Kincaid went on. 'She has the Devil's mark, and she has confessed to her crimes against God and man.' The crowd booed and screamed out threats and obscenities. Kincaid went on yelling about Elspeth's supposed crimes. Things he didn't believe, and I didn't care to hear.

This was the moment. Without turning around, I threw down my hood and shook out my hair.

Now, Hobson!

But nothing happened.

Kincaid bent and seized Elspeth by the shoulders, lifting her as if she weighed nothing at all. The crowd roared and stamped their feet on the slick cobbles.

'Where is Hobson?' I hissed, and Fionna shook her head miserably.

Elspeth was dragged behind the Maiden, her head shoved through the gap, her neck forced down on to the crossbar. A long drop of rain fell from the blade's edge on to Elspeth's bare skin and she flinched.

3

The Englishman has betrayed us. Fionna's wild eyes met mine and as one we unsheathed our weapons and pushed through the crowd. Kincaid lifted his hand to the peg that kept the blade suspended. He turned and gave a yellow-toothed grin, raising a bushy eyebrow.

'Shall I take her head?' he yelled.

The crowd screamed back 'Aye!' and I jumped over a basket of apples and came up against the wall of bodies at the base of the platform. I tried to shove them aside, but they shoved back, intent on being in the front row for the bloody sight to come ...

'John Kincaid, do not touch that peg!' I let out a moan of relief as a man in the red coat of the New Model Army stormed the stage, a musket under his arm. 'I am Lieutenant-Colonel Hobson, investigator and keeper of the peace under Lord Cromwell, Protector of the State. Cease your attack on this woman, this instant!'

Hobson, you need to work on your timing. I glanced at Fionna and pointed silently to the left side of the platform. She nodded and slipped into the crowd. I hurried towards the steps at the right, tugging my hood back up over my face.

Six of Hobson's men stormed the platform after him in their red coats, pikes and muskets held at the ready. Hobson had his orders – arrest him, attack him, whatever it took to keep Kincaid occupied while we reached our fallen sister.

'Colonel,' Kincaid said, in a wheedling voice full of false humility. 'This woman is a proven witch, as every man here can attest ... ' He looked to his jeering supporters, but the crowd had thinned considerably at the sight of the English muskets.

'Your methods are an outrage,' Hobson snarled. 'I hereby place you under arrest for the kidnap, torture and unlawful execution of fifteen innocent women.'

Hobson's soldiers slowly closed on Kincaid and he backed away. I took my chance, grabbed my skirts and climbed the steps to the platform two at a time. Elspeth had crumpled at the base of the Maiden in a heap of limbs and rags. I could reach her, if—

'No!' Kincaid screamed. 'Witch! This is your doing!'

I looked up. His eyes glared madly into mine. There was a frozen moment as the rain battered down on us, and then we both made a dash for Elspeth. He shouldered aside a musketeer who'd fumbled with his weapon. I slipped on the wet planks and fought to keep my balance. He made it to her side first. I slid to a halt as he grabbed Elspeth around the waist and yanked her to her feet.

'Stop there! All of you!' he screamed, a knife out in his hand, pressed to Elspeth's throat. 'Don't come any closer, she-devil!' His hand trembled and I froze, gripping my dagger.

'It's too late, Kincaid,' said Hobson, raising his sword. 'Kill her like that and you'll spend the rest of your days in a cell.'

Fionna vaulted up on to the platform, and hope kindled in my heart as she skidded across the wet wooden boards and into position. The third point of the triangle.

Elspeth's eyes fluttered open, and she saw Fionna and then me. Her eyes were dark and shocked but she managed to focus on me.

'Isobel . . .' I couldn't hear her voice, but I saw her cracked lips move, sounding out my name. She swallowed, her throat hitching against Kincaid's blade, and tried to mouth something else to me. But I couldn't make it out. She must have seen the lack of understanding in my eyes – she winced and her eyes rolled back in her head.

Slowly, weakly, she raised her right hand and the mark on her skin glowed violent purple in the dim evening light.

Thunder roared above us. I raised my own hand, and Fionna did the same. I felt the rush of power through my veins as if I'd been set aflame. Time seemed to slow, the rain falling to earth in a drifting curtain. Kincaid's eyes widened, and I dropped my hand to my side, drew my dagger and threw it. It scythed through the air, raindrops cartwheeling in its wake, flying straight and true towards the middle of Kincaid's forehead.

Terror was writ plain across Kincaid's face ... which shifted and changed. A patch of his skin seemed to flake away, fluttering into the air, then another, and another. His silhouette blurred. Hundreds of tiny buzzing wings opened across his body, peeling away from him until there was nothing left.

'No!' I yelled, but it was too late – my dagger flew harmlessly through the seething, buzzing cloud of moths that hung where Kincaid had been. Elspeth sank to the ground once more and Fionna sprinted to her side. The English soldiers screamed devilry and let off their muskets in fright, but their lead balls did no more harm to the demon than my dagger had. I seized one of the torches from its setting and thrust it at the insect mass. But it was too late. Kincaid was gone, his demon's form fluttering away over the rooftops and vanishing into the dark sky.

'The devil,' Hobson muttered, slack-jawed. 'You spoke the truth – the devil was here!'

I opened my mouth to snap at him that indeed, I did try to warn him, that when I said a demon plagued my homeland I meant it truly ...

Then a pain burst in my chest, as if my dagger had found my own heart, and Fionna let out a keening cry. I turned, knowing and dreading what I would see. Fionna was cradling Elspeth's limp shoulders in her lap. Her eyes were open, staring lifeless up into the sky. The rain beaded her face. Whatever she had been trying to tell me, it would remain untold.

I rushed to Fionna's side and threw my arms around her neck. She sobbed into my shoulder.

'She's gone! Her heart ... it was too much. That devil killed her, after all.' Fionna pulled away from me and looked me in the eyes, tears spilling over her cheeks.

I reached down and gently closed Elspeth's eyes, then took Fionna's hand, and Elspeth's lifeless one. Closing the circle, for the final time. 'I swear this now. I will not rest until I see justice done. Kincaid's crimes must end. We must destroy him!'

CHAPTER ONE

14 June 2014, Carriage B Seat 34

It's only a few hundred miles from London to Edinburgh. For me, that should be nothing. I kept telling myself that. Four hundred miles? Back in the States, we'd drive further for a really good taco.

My best friend, Maisie, seemed to think it was like moving to another planet. I couldn't help feeling she was right.

Cluttered English countryside streamed past my window, like an alien landscape or a glimpse into the past, with its villages, fields and bridges. Allotments, bowling greens, wenches standing at wooden gates . . . OK, maybe I'm making up the wenches, but still. I snapped a blurry photo of the rolling hills and uploaded it to Instagram.

@dihunter: I'm on my way! Edinburgh had better watch out.

I wished I felt as confident as I sounded. My phone buzzed a couple of times.

@Davekicks: @dihunter good luck! Edinburgh's a
wonderful place. Fight hard :)

That was from Sensei Dave, my ju-jitsu Master.
Ex-Master.

@tonythetigger: @dihunter you will crush it, u sparkly
diamond.

I smiled, despite the flutter of nerves in my stomach, and
messaged Tony back.

@dihunter: @tonythetigger damn right I will, tyvm u
precious cinnamon roll.

Then another reply flashed up, and I felt my heart contract
and tears prick my eyes.

Maisie had sent a picture. There was no comment, just
a photo of a room that looked like a party had exploded in
it, sticky plastic cups and icing-smeared plates and cookie
crumbs and empty bottles everywhere. And among the chaos
were all my London friends, gurning for the camera: Cheryl,
Anna, Carl looking smug in his ju-jitsu uniform, Robin and
Tony making out messily at the back, and Maisie herself
throwing up devil horns.

Grinning a slightly wobbly grin, I texted back:

Gonna miss you losers so much.

Then I put my phone away and tried not to think about all
the people I'd only get to spend virtual time with from now
on. We'd Skype and talk on the phone, sure, but it wouldn't
be the same.

I felt like I'd just got used to living in London when Dad had announced that we were moving. Again.

Leaving America had been tough enough. London was rainy and cold and laid out like someone had attached a pencil to a spider and let it wander over the map. But it had turned out to be cool and exciting and oddly familiar, like a mirror-universe New York.

I should have known our time there couldn't last. It was only a rented house in a borrowed city, a temporary stop on Dad's never-ending world tour of the weird and wacky. Maisie and the others hadn't helped when I'd told them – they'd just made jokes about kilts and castles and learning to play the bagpipes. The one thing they'd all agreed on was that it would be cold. 'Brass monkeys', Tony had said confidently.

It's supposed to be summer! I glared out of the window at the rain streaking down the window. It wasn't so much that it was raining – it rained in California, even during the summer – it was the sheer drizzly unpredictability. My train had crossed less than half the length of this soggy country and already I'd seen sheep leaning into a strong wind as if it might blow them away, bright patches of sunshine chasing across fields, mist so thick it felt like being in a video game that couldn't afford to render the world beyond the tracks. And every few minutes, another dash of raindrops against the window.

I twisted the bracelet Maisie had given me for my birthday, a circle of interwoven deer antlers that would've been really classy if it'd been made in gold and not cheap yellow plastic. I loved it, of course, but now it looked like I was having an allergic reaction or something.

I scratched at my wrist and tried not to be bitter. But it was like every time I thought I knew how I related to the world, *Dad* happened and I ended up having to reinvent myself all

11

over again, like losing a save file and having to start over from a blank page.

Except this time, the page wasn't a total blank.

I dug in my bag and pulled out the small, folded, cream-coloured piece of paper that I'd been keeping inside my book. I held it for a moment and stared out of the window. The familiar texture in my fingers was steadying. I didn't need to unfold it to know what it said, but I liked to look at the handwriting. The wild loops and sharp angles seemed friendly, somehow.

The message itself was infuriatingly vague.

Dearest Kara,

R would kill me if she knew I was writing to you, but I can't help myself. I just want you to know that I love you and I forgive you. I understand why you did it. I hope that I'll see you again someday. In the meantime, know that we will always be here on Arthur's Seat, keeping watch. Maybe one day you'll realise that you belong here too.

All my love, darling,

H

Kara was my Mom. R and H ... I had no idea.

After the funeral, Dad and Uncle Isaac went through all her things – it was too soon, but Dad said he wanted to do it and be done, like ripping off a Band-Aid. It felt more like cutting off a limb. I remember sitting out on the stoop in my itchy black skirt and my uncomfortable new black shoes, the sun setting behind the Twin Peaks while I sorted through her old hatbox of keepsakes, deciding what to keep. Meanwhile, Dad was doing what I now realise was the hard work: deciding which of her clothes and books and knick-knacks could be sold and which had to be thrown away so that we could move into the tiny apartment in the Mission where we'd spend the next two years.

Of course, this was before he'd made a fortune from death.

I'd found the envelope right at the bottom of the hatbox. Under a pile of old theatre tickets, a necklace made out of seashells, a leaflet for the youth hostel where Mom and Dad had spent their honeymoon, there had been this small creamy-coloured envelope. It was addressed to Kara Fleming, Mom's maiden name, at an address I didn't recognise.

There had been an Edinburgh postmark but no return address, and when I'd shown the letter to Dad he had been ... frustrating. No, he didn't know who H or R were. No, he didn't know what Mom was supposed to have done. No, he didn't know why she'd left Edinburgh. No, he didn't know anything about her family.

I realise that he was hurting, that he didn't want to answer a ten-year-old's endless questions about the wife he had just had to bury, especially questions he had no good answers to. But at the time, I was furious with him. How could he not know these things? She'd been his *wife*.

Whenever I was angry with him I would run to my room and start planning my escape to Edinburgh. I had elaborate plans about how I'd get there. I never thought it would actually happen.

I folded the letter carefully and slipped it back inside the cover of my book. I knew it wasn't going to be easy, but I wasn't just going to let this chance pass me by in a haze of moving and school and making new friends and learning the bus routes: I was going to find the Edinburgh my mom knew. Find out who she really was.

Maybe if I knew that, I'd be able to finally *settle*. Perhaps I would stop feeling like a butterfly in a jar, bashing against the sides of a life that was too small for me.

13

Maybe I'd even be able to sleep.

Or maybe I was putting far too much pressure on some foreign city that didn't know me and owed me nothing.

Still, at the very least I could be sure we'd have a little more privacy. It hadn't been long before Dad's fans had found out our London address, and although most of them were sweet, well-behaved English nerds, there were always a few who got carried away.

The dead birds on the doorstep had been a particular highlight. Dad laughed the whole thing off, but I found it kind of hard to talk to fans at events after that without wondering whether they had bird corpses stuffed up their sleeves, even after the police caught the guy who'd done it in the first place.

I never resented Dad's success. I remembered what it was like when we were struggling to keep a roof over our heads. For him to make his fortune doing something he loved, especially something so, well, *dorky* – I'd never begrudge anyone that. It was the weird, niche celebrity status that came with the fortune that I wasn't so keen on.

I checked Twitter again, and ...

Oh, look. They're way ahead of me.

@BBCScotland: Occult detective Jake Helsing moves to Edinburgh.

CHAPTER TWO

Thanks, BBC Scotland. Thanks a whole bunch.

Attached to the tweet was a picture of Dad at his London book launch, his hair a shaggy black mess, his glasses wonky, looking happily sheepish next to a huge pile of copies of *Outrageous Occult Occurrences – an Obsessive's Guide*.

I clicked through, and read the article. It said all the usual things: Helsing invites fans to submit stories of the supernatural in Edinburgh through his blog, Helsing will be attending events around Scotland, Helsing's new book is out now ...

I was vaguely aware of the light changing, and the train juddering and slowing as we drew up to a dim station platform.

''Scuse me,' said a voice – Scottish, male and vaguely apologetic. 'Mind if I sit here?'

I jumped, and scrambled to gather up my bag, book and water bottle which had somehow sprawled to cover the whole table in front of me.

'No, sure,' I said stiffly, though I'd rather have had the table to myself. Then I glanced up at the person I'd be sharing my table with, and my forced smile froze on my cheeks.

Holy crap. What benevolent guardian angel put a *freaking supermodel* on my train?

I looked away quick, and pretended to be very interested in my phone as he settled himself in the seat opposite me.

Eventually, as the train pulled out of the station, I snuck another look. His dark hair was clipped close to his head, which only seemed to emphasise the beautiful structure of his jaw and cheekbones, and the thickness of his eyelashes. God, they were ridiculous. I was surprised they didn't make a sound like a plane taking off when he blinked. He was about my age, I guessed, and travelling light – I didn't see him stash a bag anywhere.

He couldn't actually *be* a supermodel, not going by the clothes: jeans, a black T-shirt with a peeling band logo I didn't recognise and a thin nylon jacket. Plus, models in photos always have a slightly unreal Photoshoppy quality to them that's kind of off-putting if you look too long. I decided he was more like a movie star, whose hotness had to shine through whether they were crashing through plate glass windows or making mad passionate dialogue with their love interest.

I stared at my phone, thinking about taking a sneaky photo to text back to Maisie. *Screw the English countryside. This is what I call a view!* It would've been totally rude and awful. But this bit of excellent luck had made the world seem so much brighter, how could I not share it?

I started trying to subtly tip the phone so the camera would catch his face. I had to be careful about staring, of course. I bet he got stared at a lot. I bet he—

'Um, hullo,' he said. I looked up, met his eyes. He was

16

smiling at me, holding his hand out across the table. 'I'm Alex.'

'Oh! Uh, Diana. Helsing. Di.' *Smooth*. I shook his hand and tried not to grin *too* wide. It suddenly occurred to me to wonder how *I* looked. Probably a little rough, after last night's shenanigans, but I'd been smart enough to take my make-up off before I crashed out on Maisie's sofa, so hopefully . . .

'I think it's normal to learn someone's name before you take their photo,' he said.

I froze. Heat flooded my cheeks. I thought about denying it, but he didn't look like he was about to call the cops or anything – he was smiling. Which, newsflash, was really hot.

I winced. 'Busted! I'm sorry. How did you even know, I thought I was being totally subtle.'

'Yeah . . . no.' He laughed. 'So do you normally take pictures of people on trains? Do I have something weird on my face?'

Other than the supernatural hotness, not really . . .

'I was going to send it to my friend – I'm keeping her updated on how my journey's going.'

'OK, well,' he said, sounding as if he knew exactly why I'd been taking the photo but wasn't going to push it, 'you want to tell her a guy called Alex bought you a coffee or something? I'm away to the buffet car.'

'Oh – that's so nice! I'd really love a hot chocolate. Thank you.' I grinned. 'I'm telling her right now.'

'Back in a sec,' Alex said, and got up. I watched him walk away. Then I picked up my phone and started texting frantically, trying to describe him without sounding like I'd completely lost my mind. I also took the opportunity to cave in to vanity and check my reflection in the window. The hair was behaving itself fairly well, dark curls frizzy from the humidity but not looking like they might actually bite anyone today. Eyes not too bleary or panda-ish, no weird smudges or smears. I looked fine.

Alex reappeared with an insulated cup in each hand and a packet of shortbread balanced on one of the lids.

He smiled and sat down, pushing one of the cups towards me. 'Hot chocolate. And shortbread, to welcome you to Scotland, although I think they import this stuff from China.'

'So are you seriously going to Edinburgh without a warmer coat than that?' I asked, taking a sip of my deliciously boiling hot chocolate.

'How d'you mean?' he looked down at his thin jacket. 'You do know it's June, right?'

'Sure, June in *Scotland*,' I said. 'The single coldest place in the world, according to my friends. They said even the coal grows mould.'

'In the whole *world*? Right, that explains the polar bear infestation. These friends of yours, are they from America by any chance?'

'No,' I said smugly. 'They're Londoners, actually.'

'Oh God.' He fake-spluttered on his coffee. 'That's even worse. You need to stop hanging out with a bunch of southern pansies and get some proper Scottish friends, you'll be skipping down the Royal Mile in shorts in no time.'

I shuddered. 'Never. If this is what you call warm weather, I'm going to freeze to death by August.'

Alex grinned. 'Let me guess, you've never been to my hometown before?'

'You're from Edinburgh?' I tried not to look too much like he'd just made my day.

'Aye.' He smiled. 'And you ... I'd guess ... West Coast? Do I detect a hint of beach babe in there?'

'Like ... *dude*.' I played up to the stereotype, making him

18

laugh again. 'That's pretty good actually. Originally from San Francisco, although we've moved around a lot since then.'

'So are you moving to Edinburgh, or just visiting?'

'Moving.' I took a bite of shortbread. 'Dad's job moves around a lot, I go where he goes.'

'You don't mind?'

I shrugged. 'It's what we've always done, I guess. I mean . . . it was my sixteenth birthday yesterday so, yeah, his timing's kind of sucky.'

'Wow. Happy birthday.'

'Yep. Train ticket to a cold, wet city hundreds of miles from all my friends: not the best present I've ever gotten. But what am I going to do, run away from home? I love my dad. I probably would follow him to Antarctica, polar bears and all, if he really wanted to go. How about you?' I asked, feeling like I'd gone on about myself long enough. 'You have family in Edinburgh?'

Alex hesitated. 'No,' he said. 'No family, really.'

'Friends?' I asked, eyebrows raised. He just shook his head. *This is going well*, I thought, *He's virtually spilling his entire life story.*

'So, is it just you and your parents?' he said, overly bright and cheery, swivelling the spotlight back to me. 'Any siblings coming with you on your adventure into the great soggy unknown?'

'Just me and Dad,' I corrected gently. 'And Milly.'

'Little sister?'

'Labrador.' I grinned. 'But close enough.' That got a genuine smile out of him, so I told him all about how her full name was Millions and it was a stupid joke between Dad and me about how much it cost to keep a puppy back when Dad was a struggling bohemian ghost-hunter – although I left out the part about the ghost-hunting.

19

'If he's really a boho type you've come to Edinburgh at the right time of year,' he said. 'It's the Summer Solstice next week.'

I cringed. This, I knew – Dad's publisher was throwing him a signing-slash-Solstice-party on that night. I'd tried and failed to think of a way I could get out of going. 'Yeah, I heard. Druids, people waving around bits of twig and chanting, that sort of thing.'

'Well, maybe some of that. For people who're into that sort of thing. But the part I'm looking forward to is the Festival. They're having it on the Royal Mile. Free music, dancing, whisky, probably fire-eaters – you can't lob a brick in Edinburgh in the summer without hitting a fire-eater.'

'Sounds like fun.' I took a deep breath. 'You'll have to show me around.'

'It's a date,' he said, with a deliberate sort of smile that made me flush again, but for all the right reasons.

CHAPTER THREE

I'm alone in the dark.

If I stay still, it will get me. Somewhere ahead of me freedom is waiting. If I just keep moving, if I'm careful enough, quick enough, brave enough, I know I can escape this place.

I walk forward.

I can feel things hanging all around me in the darkness.

Some instinct pulls me to step to the side. I walk on.

I feel cold metal drag across my shoulder, tearing the skin, and a high-pitched shriek goes up as something flutters past my face.

Light flares, all around me, flickering and yellow.

The light is worse than the darkness.

Long, thick needles and knives hang all around me, each one covered in a mass of giant black hawkmoths. Their wings twitch and flutter open, splintering the white skull markings on their backs.

The needles twist and spin as the moths take flight, hundreds, thousands, fluttering and shrieking. The knives are knocked swinging and I throw up my arms to shield my face. The skin is already pocked and bleeding. I look down and I can see my scraped knees, the ruin that used to be my toes. The moths crowd in on me, beating around my head and screaming into my ears, and I throw my head down and run, it never helps but I always run, and the needles lunge at me out of the darkness ahead, pricking across my bare shoulders, my neck, my scalp and my arms.

The hawkmoths keep up their awful sound, skree skree skree skree, *and then I see it right ahead – I always see it – a blade as wide as my shoulders, black with blood, hanging in the air. I can't avoid it. I can't stop.*

I try to open my eyes, and everything is so bright, and there's something reaching for me – bleached bone fingertips clawing for my shoulder, the empty eye sockets of a grinning skull looming above me.

I woke screaming, hardly aware where I was. A moving sensation beneath my body, a face opposite, mouth hanging open.

Alex. Oh God.

I was on the train, my sweat-slick hands clutching at the armrest.

'Di! Diana, it's OK,' Alex was saying, in that voice, the one people always use when they're not totally sure if it is OK but they're really hoping that saying it will make it so.

I sat up straight, and tried to smile while my insides turned to churning lava, leaving me a burned-out, red-hot shell of embarrassment.

'I'm fine, I'm sorry,' I said. My throat felt dry. Like I'd been yelling. I shifted in my seat, and the rest of the train pulled back into focus. It wasn't just Alex who was staring at me. Across the aisle, an old lady and a man in a suit were both wearing concerned frowns. 'Sorry,' I muttered again.

'You were ... um ...' Alex started, sitting back in his seat. 'Bad dream?'

I tried to clear my throat. I couldn't meet his eyes. 'Yeah. I . . . I think I'll go splash some water on my face or something.'

I clambered out of my seat and stumbled down the aisle without looking back, smacking my knee painfully on one of the armrests, but I didn't stop walking, even though the train seemed to be constricting around me, conspiring to block my path . . .

Calm down, Jeez. The train is not out to get you.

I locked myself in the nasty, cramped bathroom, put down the toilet lid and sat there with my hands over my mouth, bracing myself against the urge to cry. Dry-eyed, I stared at the damp floor and let out a lacklustre stream of cursing. Swearing it out always made me feel a little better, after I'd had the dream: I guess it felt like proof that I was still me, still living in the real world.

It was pretty cold comfort this time, though. Talk about a real *nightmare*.

How can I go back out there? How can I sit across from him for another hour after this? He's going to think I'm nuts.

Well, to be fair: I am a little nuts.

I splashed my face and went back, my spine straight and a sheepish smile curling the corners of my lips. I knew if I styled it out, played OK, sooner or later I would forget that my composure had started out as a lie.

They say a person can get used to almost anything, and sometimes I felt like I was living proof. I'd had the same dream, nearly every night, for *five years*.

Therapy didn't shift it, nor did hypnosis. I'd taken drugs to make me sleep and drugs to keep me awake. I'd meditated, prayed, and I'd even been exorcised – when you live with a ghost-hunter, it would be silly not to at least try it. I'd seen too much, through Dad's investigations, not to believe there

23

were things in the world beyond our understanding, even if I didn't know exactly what they were.

But nothing worked. The dream lingered.

When I got back to my seat, there was a fresh cup of coffee waiting for me, and another packet of cookies. They were oat ones this time.

I kept my cool, but inside I was a suddenly a whole new kind of mess.

You are perfect. You know that? I could kiss you ...

Now, there was a thought to distract a girl from her crazy.

I sat down and pulled the coffee towards me, cupping it between my hands. 'Thank you. So much.'

'Well, you seemed like you didn't want to drop off again.' Alex smiled. 'You ... you don't have to tell me, but that seemed pretty unpleasant. You sure you're OK?'

'I'm fine,' I insisted.

But then something weird happened: I felt like I *could* tell him. Even weirder, I felt like maybe I wanted to.

'It's this recurring dream I have,' I blurted, before I could second-guess myself. 'Have done since I was a kid. It's a bit ... dark. There are all these moths ... you know those huge ones, long as your hand, with markings like a skull on their backs? *Those*. And there are things hanging from the ceiling ... knives and stuff. And it's dark, and ... it's just really creepy.' I watched his face, and just for a moment there was a flicker, like the light in his eyes dimmed. *Crap, I was wrong, he's going to go all quiet and awkward and run away from me as fast as his sculpted calves can take him ...*

But then he seemed to come back to himself. 'Moths and knives? Wow. That sounds pretty awful.'

'Also, just for a minute I thought you were a skeleton!' I said, forcing a smile. 'I kind of half woke up and I saw you, only you were all just bones. That was new. Nuts, right?'

24

He gave me a kind of slow-blink, head-tilt smile. It was impossible to tell what he thought and I felt the blood rush to my cheeks.

Conversation kind of ran out after that. Which was understandable. I'd just told him he looked like the living dead, after all. I drank my coffee and stared out of the window as we passed through a small town with tall brown stone houses and a row of old factories along the train tracks. Their windows were broken now, and scrawls of graffiti climbed their walls like trailing vines.

Alex yawned hugely. 'Actually, I didn't sleep so well last night – a little micro-sleep sounds pretty great right now.'

'Hey, don't let me stop you.' I shrugged. 'And I promise if you start thrashing I'll wake you up. One good turn, right?'

He grinned, pulled his hood up over his head and twisted away from me, shutting his eyes and resting his head on the seat back.

I plugged in my headphones and grabbed my book, letting myself vanish into the music and the words. I actually managed to lose track of time, so when I caught the words 'terminates here' on the train announcements I sat up almost as suddenly as if I'd been dreaming and scrambled to get my things together.

Alex's eyes blinked open.

'Uh? Oh! Home sweet home,' he said. He nodded out of the window. We were slowing down, travelling through a deep cutting between tall buildings. The rain had stopped and shafts of weak sunlight were spearing through the clouds. I looked up at them and felt my heart lift slightly. There was hope for a sunny day, somewhere behind all this grey.

I smiled over at Alex, too. I couldn't help feeling like Edinburgh was a little less of a mystery now that I knew someone there, even though I didn't really *know* him yet.

We pulled into a cavernous station. It felt pretty much like the big London train stations – all exposed steel and concrete.

Alex stood by while I shoved my things into my bag, and we disembarked together.

'So, where in Edinburgh do you live?' I asked, as we strolled side by side towards the ticket barrier at the end of the platform. 'Not that I'm gonna have any idea where anything is for a couple of weeks.'

'In the centre,' Alex said with a smile.

'Good answer,' I laughed. I fished my ticket from my pocket and let myself out on to the station concourse, with its generic British shops and ticket queues – all still reassuringly familiar, except that the gift shop we passed was full of tartan and whisky, instead of Union Jacks and postcards of Big Ben.

Dad had said he'd meet me at the top of the escalator to Princes Street, but of course, when we got to the top and stepped out into the glass and concrete shelter, there was no sign of him.

'Typical,' I said, getting out my phone. I texted him:

I'm at the station, are you on your way?

'Want me to wait with you?' Alex asked.

'Oh it's fine. I'm sure he'll be along in a minute,' I said, and then wished I could step outside my body for a moment so I could literally kick myself. What the hell did I say that for? Dad's lateness was legendary, and this boy with a face like the Angel of Cool Explosions had offered to stand here with me until he arrived and *I'd told him no*.

'I'll see you later, then. I hope you like your new house. Pat Milly for me,' he said. 'Oh, and, Diana – happy birthday.'

It was odd, the way he said *happy birthday* ... it sounded oddly serious, but before I could puzzle out whether it'd sounded more like *deepest condolences* or *will you marry me*, he'd waved, grinned and walked off.

I stood for a moment, watching him go, then checking my phone for any word from Dad, before I realised my mistake.

'Crap!' I said aloud, drawing stares from the other people struggling out of the station with their suitcases dragging behind them.

I didn't get his phone number.

CHAPTER FOUR

I sat in the Starbucks inside Edinburgh Waverley station for a while, nursing a steaming mocha with extra whipped cream and obsessively refreshing my emails. I tried not to stew over my ability to snatch dating defeat from the jaws of victory, but it certainly wasn't helping my mood.

I cycled through every source my dad could possibly have used to contact me: missed calls, texts, Twitter, Facebook, emails ... but there was nothing.

I swigged back the last chocolatey dregs of my mocha and sighed. I wasn't worried about Dad. He'd probably just fallen down a research hole and lost all track of time, digging through old books or scouring the obscure corners of the internet for background on one of his supposed hauntings. His phone would probably be buried under piles of unreliable witness statements.

I hitched my bag on to my shoulder and sent one final text:

Getting a cab, if you never see me again I've been murdered.

My taxi driver started talking as soon as we'd navigated the tricky exit to the station. 'So, New Town, eh? Nice area. Should be there in about ten minutes. Visiting for the summer?'

'Actually, I'm moving here. My dad's job is here.' I settled back against the squishy leather seat and stared out of the window. We'd taken a sharp left turn and stopped in traffic on the main road. *So this is where I'm moving to.*

For a start, there was a castle. An absolutely genuine, absolutely *enormous* castle just sitting there in the middle of the city, spitting distance from the train station and the glossy shopping street. The clouds had cleared a little to let the late afternoon sunlight through and it glinted on wet brown stone, Victorian brick, glass and concrete. Running beside the road on my left side, I found myself looking down a steep slope into – well, in California we would've called it a ravine. A deep chasm in the middle of the city that seemed to contain a damp-looking park with winding paths and soggy benches.

It gave me the strangest feeling, something I couldn't quite put my finger on. The view was so incredibly foreign that it took me a second to realise the feeling was *familiarity*.

Did Mom see this same view? Did she walk in that park and gaze at the castle and shop in the stores along this road?

I hadn't seen so much *geography* right in the middle of an urban environment for years. Not since we left San Francisco, where the streets undulated like roller-coaster tracks towards the sea.

I guess the driver must've seen me staring intensely out of the window, drinking in the craggy landscape.

'First time in Edinburgh?' he asked.

'Uh-huh.'

'You're going to love it,' he said, with genuine-sounding enthusiasm. 'Best place on earth.'

I thought that might be pushing it a *little*, but I met his eyes in the rear-view mirror and smiled. 'It ... I mean, this is going to be a really dumb thing to say, but it all looks so *old*. Even the stuff that's not that old. You know?'

The driver laughed. 'Aye, history is sort of catching around here. People have been living on the Castle rock since a thousand BC, probably longer.'

I was starting to see why Dad wanted to come here. Until now, I couldn't imagine how *anywhere* could have more dark corners of history for him to explore than London, where murder and mayhem were layered in the bedrock. But I could see that three thousand years of occupation would be plenty for him to get his teeth into.

'So, Helsing, eh? Don't mean to pry, but I saw it on your email, there.'

Oh, right. I'd shown him the printed-out emergency copy of the email Dad had sent with our new address, which had my name right at the top. I flushed slightly.

'I had that ghost-hunter in my cab the other day,' the driver went on. 'Jake Helsing. Unusual name. Any relation?'

I briefly weighed the possibility of outright lying, but it didn't seem worth the trouble. 'Wow, that's a coincidence,' I said. 'He's my dad.'

I saw the driver's eyebrows shoot up in the rear-view mirror. 'What's that like? Having a ghostbuster for a dad? Any plans to go into the family business?'

'Not really,' I said, with a semi-apologetic smile. 'I don't have the patience for it.'

'You know, Edinburgh's one of the most haunted places in the world,' he said proudly. 'I've had my fair share of contact with the other side. My sister's boyfriend got bitten by a ghost, right on the ear! A couple of years ago, it was ...'

I could tell this was going to go on for a while. This was

why I didn't usually talk about Dad's job. It's not that I'm embarrassed, and it's not even that I don't believe. I've seen some stuff I can't explain too – even if you discount the freakish dreams as lingering post-bereavement trauma or some other psych-speak. It's just that once you reveal you know a real-life ghost-hunter, 99 per cent of people will want to tell you all about their own encounter with the supernatural.

I don't mind what people believe they've seen. I only wish they didn't feel the need to tell me about it.

'... turns out, she was a lady of ill repute from the seventeenth century, murdered in that very pub. Nasty business. Now she goes around biting any man who spends too much time there.'

That sounded pretty reasonable to me. Classic revenge tale, one of the five major UFBs – unfinished businesses. I could rattle them off as easy as breathing: revenge, closure, recognition, an unfinished mission, or protection of a loved one. This pub prostitute was clearly a revenge-orientated ghost, and as long as she was only giving guys non-lethal nips on the ear, as far as I was concerned she was well within her rights.

My phone buzzed. It was a text from Dad, finally.

Diana!!! So sorry, hon, phone was off. You OK? ETA?

I started to type out 'I'm fine', then changed my mind.

Argh argh help I'm being murdered.

Har har. See you soon.

'... was on the radio just before you got in, that's a chilling piece of work. Right in the museum like that! Awful. Anyway,

31

here we are,' the driver said, segueing so smoothly from his ghost story to my destination that it made me double-take.

We turned a sharp corner, and I looked out of the window again. Oh yes, we'd definitely arrived – I'd checked out my new home on Street View, and found that when they said Royal Circle they really meant the circle part. Two perfect Georgian crescents formed a circle around a small green park bordered by iron railings. The buildings were tall townhouses in brown stone with glossy painted doors and sash windows, exactly the kind of house that Jane Austen heroines visited when they came to Town for the season, although the Town was usually London or Bath. And usually they regretted it.

The taxi rolled to a halt and I gave the driver the last of my cash, and thanked him for the story, because I might as well. It wasn't as if he could corner me and insist on telling another.

'You should tell your dad about it.' He grinned. 'Might make for a good chapter for the next book, eh?'

'I will. He might look into it.' I meant it, too. Dad had a genuinely, bizarrely bottomless appetite for ghost stories, whether they seemed vaguely plausible or not.

The driver waved as he drove off, and I waved back and then turned and took a longer look at the house.

Number sixteen had sandstone steps like a little bridge leading up to a green door with a brass handle. The green door was all that distinguished it from the houses on either side – they all had identical dark windows, four storeys above ground and a basement floor that you could get to from the pavement if you were willing to risk the steep descent down some scary iron steps.

The sky had clouded over again and now rain was pattering down. My scalp prickled as my hair curled tighter in the insidious wetness.

I fumbled my key into the lock and the door opened into a cold, echoey hallway.

It was a little bit like travelling through time – from Georgian elegance to ultra-modern swank. The stairs were polished wood and brass, the walls were white except for a deep blue accent wall that ran up the side of the stairs. Probably antique tables stood by the walls, their effect slightly spoiled by the piles of soggy cardboard boxes that'd been stacked on top of them.

'Dad?' I called. There was no reply. But then I heard one of the most comforting sounds in the world, at least to a dog-owner: the scrabbly, breathy sound of an overexcited Labrador coming down a flight of stairs at near-terminal velocity.

Milly scrambled to the ground, charged across the tiles and leaped up to plant her paws on my chest, her tail wagging a million miles an hour, pure slobbery joy on her fuzzy golden face.

'Hi, Milly! Hi! You wanna let me in, huh, silly dog?' I shut the door behind me and knelt down to give her a hug, getting a big slobbery lick and then a whack on the face with her tail for my trouble. 'Where's Dad, huh?' I asked, scratching behind her ears. 'Where's that silly old nerd now?'

Milly obediently let out an eardrum-rattling bark and shot off down the hall, towards what looked like it might be the kitchen.

I peeled off my coat and hung it over the bannisters before I followed her, glancing in through the doors leading off the hall as I passed. One was a living room with soft, brand-new looking teal-coloured sofas pointing towards a fireplace and an enormous, slightly curved TV screen. The next had empty floor-to-ceiling shelves on all the walls, comfy-looking armchairs and a big oak desk by the back window.

33

'Holy crap, Milly,' I muttered, although she had already vanished down the hall. 'Never lived somewhere with a *library* before ...' I tore myself away and followed Milly into the kitchen, which seemed like it'd been beamed in from the Starship *Enterprise* – the lens-flare reboot, not the 1960s one made of cardboard and string. I turned to fully take in the gleaming sci-fi design and found myself looking at a doorway and a flight of dark stairs heading down.

Milly was sitting in front of it, panting smugly.

Of course. What could be more Dad than lurking in a Georgian basement? I wondered if he'd started unpacking his skulls yet.

The basement stairs were decorated with Victorian Gothic black and grey flock wallpaper, and I grinned as I walked down them. *So Dad*. He couldn't possibly have had time to decorate in the day and a half he'd been here before me, so it must have come with the house. I wouldn't have been surprised to hear it'd been a major factor in him renting this place.

At the bottom, enough cardboard boxes and plastic packing crates to build a good-sized fort were stacked around the walls of a large room with wood-panelled walls and soft brown carpet. Gleaming brass pipes ran to a huge antique sink and cast iron oven range in one corner.

Dad's old study desk sat in the opposite corner, scratched and pockmarked and stained from decades of writerly frustration. Sure enough, a box was open on top and one of the skulls – I think it was George – had been taken out and given pride of place on the windowsill that looked out on to the steps down from the street.

Dad, on the other hand, sat in the middle of the room on a cardboard box, hunched over his laptop, which was resting on another cardboard box. One of his huge old occult books was lying on the floor by his foot, which tapped restlessly on the cracked and gold-embossed leather as he typed.

'Hi, Dad,' I said cheerily.

'Diana!' He leaped up, almost toppling his laptop, and climbed over the boxes and piles of books to pull me into a tight hug. 'I didn't hear you come in! Sorry about the train. How was the journey?'

'It was fine,' I said. *I actually got a date with a really hot boy, and then dreamed in front of a bunch of strangers, and then I let him walk off without getting his number*. It was such a ridiculous chain of events, I couldn't bring myself to mention any of it.

'And the party? Not too hungover?'

I rolled my eyes at him. 'Dad,' I complained.

'Good, good, great, excellent,' Dad said, ruffling my hair in the way he knows I hate, and then sat back down on his box.

'So, what's happening on the internet that's so absorbing you forgot all about me?' I asked, dragging my fingers through my hair.

'It's *very* interesting,' Dad said, without irony, and his voice took on the slow, thoughtful tone he got when he was telling a story. 'Barely an hour ago, in this very city, a normal family of tourists were visiting the National Museum of Scotland. It was a rainy Saturday afternoon, and the place was busy.' It was tempting to interrupt him with a *Dad, I know what day it is*, but he'd gone on before I could butt in. 'They were in the Grand Gallery when it happened. They had just turned away, shuddering, from a seventeenth-century guillotine called the Maiden when their young son tugged on his mother's sleeve. When she turned around, he held up something in both hands. Something rotten and shrivelled.'

Dad raised his hands in front of him, cupping something imaginary a little smaller than a basketball. I shuddered, just a little, despite myself.

35

'An ancient, severed head. At first, his mother assumed it was a prop – it was too disgusting, too ragged to be an exhibit. Then, she caught the smell. She asked him where he found it, and he pointed to the Maiden. He said the horrible old man had just put it there. Reluctantly, she took it from him. It was soft. *Squishy*.'

Dad's fingers twitched, squishing into the flesh of the imaginary severed head. I didn't dignify that with the disgusted response he was looking for, but my skin crawled.

'They took it to Museum security, who confirmed it was a genuine human head – and *not* one from their collection. The police are looking for the man who placed the head on the Maiden, but the little boy will only say that he was old and horrible, that he had yellow fingernails and yellow teeth, and he was wearing black.'

'Well, that's awful.'

'Isn't it?' Dad beamed. 'Obviously, the police are saying it's a disgusting prank, but I really think this could be a haunting. That old man might have been an executioner, or even a victim! That could have been *his own head*! I knew we were right to come here, this story is going to be huge, mark my words.'

I gave him a slow, sarcastic two-thumbs-up. 'Severed heads. Best Day Ever. I'm gonna leave you to it.'

'Your room's at the top of the house,' Dad said, his attention already hooked back on the screen. 'Yeah. This is going to be great.'

I couldn't help thinking the little kid and his mother who'd actually found the thing weren't having such a great day. But, ghoulish excitement aside, at least I knew Dad would try to help them, if he could. After all, that's what he always said ghost-hunting was really all about: a listening ear and an open mind.

Of course, sometimes it was more about an eye on the door and the police on speed-dial. We'd dealt with plenty of people who really should've called a doctor before they called a ghost-hunter.

I headed up the stairs, and up, and up again. I didn't know what Dad was thinking, renting this place – it was so much bigger than we needed! My footsteps were silent on the plushly carpeted stairs as I climbed. I paused on the third floor and opened a door at random to find a bathroom nearly as big as our San Francisco apartment, with elegant turquoise glass vases and matching, fluffy-looking towels, and even turquoise soap in a dispenser over the sink.

How long would it take for this place to feel like home? I was starting to feel like I was trespassing here, like the curious girl in the beginning of a fairy tale, but not the kind where she marries the prince and lives happily ever after – more like the type where she finally opens the forbidden door and finds his previous wives dangling from butcher's hooks on the other side.

There was only one door on the fourth floor, at the very top of the stairs. I pushed it open, and caught a glimpse of an attic room with a large skylight before I heard a sound and froze.

Skree. Skree skree.

My palm went slick on the doorknob.

I knew that sound. It was the high-pitched shriek of a hawkmoth.

CHAPTER FIVE

Cold sweat trickled down my back.

I wasn't sure how long I had been standing there in the doorway.

The sound was *still going on*. The harsh squeak – *skree skree skree skree*.

I planted my hands over my ears. A distressed whine escaped from the back of my throat.

I could run. Could just go. Leave the room, leave this house, leave Dad, and run.

No! This is my home now, whether I chose it or not. This city was my mother's home. And I won't by driven out by ... by ...

I swallowed and slowly lowered my hands into ready stance. In some part of my brain that wasn't flooded with adrenaline, I knew it was irrational, that I was inching into a completely empty room, fists up as if I was expecting to be tackled by an opponent I could punch out.

Still, I held my stance and it gave me courage. Sensei Dave would be proud.

The room was over-designed, just like the rest, statement walls and art and everything matching. Bed. Desk. Skylight windows. Giant wardrobe that could have led straight to Narnia. Boxes of my stuff, some already opened.

There was nothing strange here, except for the noise.

Skree! Skree skree skree ...

It was coming from the wardrobe.

Feeling sick and helpless, I grabbed a wooden hanger that'd been left on the bed, kicked aside an empty box marked 'DI CLOTHES' and hooked the hanger around the wardrobe's handle.

I pulled, very slowly.

Something brown and about the length of my index finger crawled out of the wardrobe. And then another. And another.

I shrieked and let go of the hanger and backed away. The wardrobe door swung slowly, inexorably open. Moths the size of small birds swarmed all over the wardrobe and all over my clothes, chittering and squeaking, flicking their brown and yellow wings as they crawled out into the room.

Tears scorched down my cheeks and I staggered back, the world blurring in front of me.

Not happening, not happening, this is not ... it's not ...

But it was. They were here. In the real world. In my bedroom.

Something buzzed past my ear, and I screamed and flailed, and the back of my hand slapped something in mid-air. It fell, landing at my feet. It was so real – brown and black, with the white splotch on its back that looked like a human skull. I drew back a foot and punted it away from me with a disgusted '*Gneeeeah!*' It hit the far wall with a soft thump.

I cast around for something I could use to swat a thousand shrieking hawkmoths. In the end, I dived for the bed and seized one of the thick pillows, and wrenched open the skylight window above my head. Perhaps I could bully them out with the pillow . . .

The moths took flight all at once, spinning into a dark cloud that rose up from the wardrobe like a tornado and swarmed right towards me, still shrieking.

I crouched and curled into a ball, holding the pillow over my head, bracing myself for the blanket of insects choking and devouring . . .

Instead, I heard the thudding of wings on glass. I lowered the pillow in time to see the last few moths swirling up through the open window and out into the grey sky. The one I'd kicked across the room was the last to get out – it twitched and spun in the air, and then it was gone.

I huddled there on the floor for a moment. A few drops of freezing rain dripped from the window and landed in my hair. Apart from the rattle of water on the glass, there was no sound but the rasp of my own breath.

They'd all gone. All at once. As if they were all one creature, responding to a single command – or as if I had imagined them. Perhaps I really had gone nuts.

But a single glance at the wardrobe told a different story.

My clothes – oh-so-thoughtfully unpacked into the wardrobe for me – hung haphazardly off their hangers or were strewn across the floor, dotted with ragged holes the size of pound coins.

I struggled to my feet. My gaze darted around the room, seeing moths in every shadow. I circled crazily, kicking furniture, pulling out drawers, even bending down to look under the bed, before I was finally forced to approach the wardrobe.

I grabbed the hanger again and used it to poke through the clothes, stabbing into the darkness and pulling out torn-up shirts and pants and skirts and dresses and jackets.

My gym bag was right at the bottom, its plastic coating slightly chewed, but when I opened it up my gi was still intact, and my sweatpants and gym T-shirt too.

Everything else, my entire wardrobe, from my beautiful silk bridesmaid's dress to my fox onesie, was now riddled with holes.

I teared up again. My nightmare had come to life, or at least part of it ... and it had eaten all my clothes? It just seemed so ... *petty*.

I was gingerly pushing my dresses aside when I saw something on the back of the wardrobe, lighter than the rest of the wood. I recoiled, but it didn't move. It was a scratch in the dark wood ... but too regular, too recognisable to be an accident.

It was in the shape of an 'R'.

There were more letters. I parted the hangers and stared at the words that had been scratched into the back of my wardrobe. The handwriting was spiky, and the letters were torn out of the wood leaving rough and splintered edges, as if someone had been in a hurry to get their message across. Which was odd, because the message itself made no sense.

The Witch Pricker Returns

I stared, so nonplussed that the whole thing lost some of its creep-factor.

I'd seen some crazy stuff on my travels. But this spooky bullshit had just leapfrogged right to the top of the list. I sat down heavily on the bed, my hands shaking in my lap as I stared at the words in the wardrobe.

Take the most likely explanation. Extrapolate. What do you get?

I was being haunted. There was something in this house – in this room? In the wardrobe? – that wanted to frighten me.

But ... 'The Witch Pricker Returns'? Was that supposed to mean something to me?

41

'A+ for presentation,' I muttered, summoning up every bit of snark I had left. 'D- for content. Solid C effort.' I scooped up a moth-eaten T-shirt and my gym bag in one shaking hand and grabbed one of my boxes of belongings under the other arm, and left the room, closing the door behind me.

Dad was in the Starship Kitchen now, his laptop set up on the counter and his bag of occult tricks unpacked all over the kitchen table.

'It's seventeenth century!' Dad called over to me when he noticed I'd walked in.

'I . . . what?' I blinked.

'The head, from the museum!' Dad beamed. 'They just confirmed it. The head's genuine, and it's *old*.'

'Oh, great,' I said, feeling slightly hysterical. 'I'm real happy for them. Dad, I have to show you something.' I held out the T-shirt in front of me, riddled with holes. Dad didn't look at it.

'Hmm?' he said, turning back to tap something on his laptop.

'Dad, something really freakish is happening. Right here, in the house.' I twisted the shirt in my hands. 'I think my room might be haunted.'

That did at least get his attention.

'Di, I don't have time for pranks right now,' he said.

'I haven't pranked you since I was thirteen! I'm deadly serious.' I could hear my own voice shaking. 'Moths, Dad,' I said, high-pitched and squeaky with nerves. 'Gnarly death's head hawkmoths the size of my *hand*, just like in my nightmare, hundreds of them! They were in my closet. They ate everything, and they left this weird message and . . .'

'Sweetie,' Dad said, in a voice of infinite patience. That single word gave me creeps not quite like any creeps I'd had before.

42

He didn't believe me.

My own dad, Jake Helsing, the famous ghost-hunter. My dad, who would listen to any ghost story from any random stranger. My dad, who had made his fortune listening to them. He wasn't listening to me.

'I'll come and take a look if you want,' Dad went on, giving me what I bet he thought was a piercing stare. 'But I'm just not in the mood for games, right now, there's so much to do, and this head thing could actually *be* something. You still want me to come?'

I stared at him for a second.

You know what? Screw you, Dad. I twisted the T-shirt harder in my hands. *This is important! This is real!*

But I don't want your help if you're going to be like this.

'No, never mind,' I told him. 'I wouldn't want you to have to look away from Twitter for five minutes.'

'Of course,' he said, with a theatrical wink. I swallowed my frustration. 'I'm really sorry about your clothes – maybe the moths got to them while they were in storage. You should go out tomorrow and treat yourself to a whole new wardrobe, I'll give you some birthday money.'

'Sure,' I said hollowly. 'And I'm going to move my stuff down to one of the spare bedrooms. I don't like the attic.' *There is no way in hell I am sleeping in that room.*

'Take your pick, we have about ten. Oh, and I found a ju-jitsu club,' he added. 'There's a leaflet on the hall table.'

'Sure. Thanks.'

I turned on my heel and left him to his research, traitorous tears pricking at the corner of my eyes.

All my life – when Mom died, when we moved continents, when I had nothing else to hold on to – I always had my Dad.

Now, for the first time ever, I felt utterly alone.

43

CHAPTER SIX

The martial arts school Dad had found turned out to be a converted church. I stood outside it for a moment, the morning after my encounter with the moths, wringing out my wet hair as best I could. I stared up at the arched and barred windows, and the worn faces of gargoyles peering down at me from the roof gutter, dribbling rainwater down the old grey stone.

I had slept badly. No more moths in my closets, no more messages – nothing out of the ordinary at all. Only another dream, horrifying but sadly predictable. It had been a bad one. I'd woken at 4 a.m. in an unfamiliar room that stank of bug spray and fresh paint, with the taste of blood in my mouth, and lain awake until sunrise.

But as I gazed up at the church, I felt fine. A little jumpy from lack of sleep, but fine.

The most credible of Dad's interview subjects usually said they felt almost guilty for going on with their real lives after something bizarre had happened to them, as if they felt that they were *supposed* to completely fall apart, or run, or even spontaneously fall down dead. But that's just not how it works. You see a ghost ... and then you have to go to work, and take your kids to school, and watch television. Mostly, you're fine.

I just needed to work out some of the tension that'd gripped my shoulders and my back.

And, to be fair to Dad, he had found the perfect place.

I'd joined enough new dojos to know that there was no way of predicting what they would be like. Some took place in sports centres, some in converted rooms above coffee shops, some in school halls. Sometimes there was lots of bowing, sometimes half the class was in Japanese. Sometimes there was lots of laughter; other classes were deadly serious. You just never knew.

It was a weird feeling to push through the big oak doors and find myself in a church, under vaulted eaves, with stained glass saints looking in through the windows at the group of people in gi – kimono-style wrap jackets and loose trousers – preparing to step on to the tatami mats where the pews would once have been.

A tall, bald black belt was helping one of the white belts with their warm-up, and he turned to see me come in and smiled.

'Hi,' I said, 'I'm Di Helsing, I called yesterday ...'

'Of course, welcome.' He offered me his hand. 'I'm Master Yeun's assistant. You said you have your own gi?'

'Yes.' I shifted my gym bag on my shoulder.

'Well, there's a changing room just through there, and warm-up starts in five minutes.'

I gave him a grin and headed in the direction he'd pointed, through a door I was pretty sure would have led to the vestry when this was a church. Inside, I found a small room, crowded with lockers and a wooden bench, with the world's tiniest shower cubicle crammed into one corner. I stripped off my tracksuit bottoms and T-shirt – the only clothes I had left, unless I wanted to rock up to ju-jitsu class wearing yesterday's post-party outfit – and pulled out my gi.

It was bright white, a little soft with age and use but meticulously clean. I slipped on the vest top I wore underneath, pulled on the white pants and did up the drawstring. Then I wrapped myself in the jacket, crossing the lapels left over right and winding my brown belt around my waist.

The familiar ritual was comforting. No matter where I was, how bad my dreams, whatever else was happening in my life, when I was wearing my gi I felt ... *strong*. Not just physically, although it certainly didn't hurt to know I could hold my own in a fight. When I was wearing my gi and my belt, I felt like I was a part of something. I represented something – the sport, the teachings of all the masters who'd gone before me, the history. It was only cotton, but it felt like plate armour.

I bullied my wet and frizzy hair into a ponytail and threw my shoulders back in my best impression of a confident person before walking back into the church to meet my new classmates.

It was a mixed-ability class, and I spotted two other brown belts: one of them was an old black lady with grey hair cropped short against her skull, and the other was a tall white girl with thick, strawberry-blonde hair.

There were several white, blue and purple belts too. They were all wearing matching blue gi, and I felt myself flush as the tall blonde girl turned to glance at me in my bright white outfit.

There was a sudden hush, and I turned to see a middle-aged Korean lady I recognised from the club's flyer stepping into the church. My eyes flicked to her belt, and felt a thrill of excitement – she was wearing a black belt wrapped in red and striped to indicate she was a Master.

She clapped her hands. 'Class, form up in belt order, white at the front, black at the back.'

We lined up, bowed as we stepped on to the mat, and then turned to face the Master and bowed to her.

'We have a visiting student today. Miss Diana Helsing.' She gestured to me, and the other students turned. 'I am Master Yeun. Welcome.'

'Thank you,' I said, bowing. Master Yeun bowed back.

As Master Yeun started to lead the class in a warm-up, I relaxed into the rhythm of the lesson, spending all my breath and attention on keeping up. It was like meditation, except that it left me sweating, out of breath, exhilarated and occasionally bruised.

This was always how I felt most like myself, but I needed it today more than ever. I twitched at the squeaking sound of a student's heel turning on the floor. I almost lost my balance when a draught blew over the back of my neck and the dream elbowed its way suddenly into my thoughts.

After an intense warm-up and a few kick drills, Master Yeun told us to put on our gloves and pair up for sparring and throwing practice. My partner-slash-opponent was one of the other brown belts, the one with the thick blonde hair. I looked her over more closely as we squared up to each other.

Her hair was tied up in a high ponytail to expose a clipped-short undercut. If this was a real fight, I would have been able to catch her hair and pull it, but probably not as easily as she could catch me by my curls. She had a good couple of inches of height on me – but that's not necessarily good in ju-jitsu. The shorter and heavier you are, the harder it is for your opponent to toss you around. At a guess we'd probably be in the same weight class, but hers was all spread out. Per square inch, I had the advantage.

'Fight!' Master Yeun called.

We bowed, our eyes locked, and she grinned widely as we started to circle each other.

I breathed deeply and evenly, a real calm finally descending as I tuned my thoughts in to her body, where she was moving, the tiny movements of her arms that would telegraph that she was planning to strike ...

So I saw her hips roll before her leg came up in an attempt at a front side-kick, and I was ready for it, blocking with my right arm and dodging away. I smiled, pleased to have denied her the first strike, but I couldn't lose focus. She had the longer reach, so I had to stay back unless I wanted her to decide when we hit the mat. Her left hand was high, so I spun and aimed a solid heel-strike to her left leg. It struck home and she staggered back, but her eyes lit up and she came at me again almost immediately.

We were pretty evenly matched. With every movement, each strike and breath and twist and burst of pain, I felt lighter in my heart, as if I could expel the tensions of ghosts and dreams and Dad and everything through my fists.

My blonde opponent got me hard in the shoulder with a punch, and I ducked under her arm and grabbed her into a shoulder lock, kicked against the back of her knee and bore her to the ground.

She hit hard with a soft 'oof!', but lost no time rolling over. I tried to brace myself, to keep her under my weight, but I was off-balance from the throw and we grappled for a minute, rolling and twisting on the tatami mat. Everything went out of my head then, except the urge to *win*. I heard the sounds of other students hitting the ground, getting up, tapping out. Then I spotted my chance and sprung an arm-bar on her, pulling her wrist towards me and then swinging my legs over her chest to keep the rest of her down. She was stuck.

'OK, tap!' she gasped, both hands too pinned to strike the mat. I let go at once and leaned back on my elbows, catching my breath, the thrill of victory squirming in my chest like a blissed-out puppy. My opponent rolled to her knees, staring at me with an odd expression on her face – her mouth was smiling, but there was a frown creasing between her eyebrows.

I was just starting to get to my feet, to offer her a rematch, when Master Yeun called out '*Yame!*' and the students all stopped sparring and clambered to their feet or brushed down their gi, panting. 'Good work everyone, get a drink of water and adjust your gi and then back here for the warm-down. Good work, Miss Helsing,' she added. I beamed at the praise, and bowed just to be safe, then offered my hand to the blonde girl to shake. She hesitated a split second, staring at it, before she shook.

'You're good,' she said, as we got to our feet together.

'You too,' I panted.

'Do something to your hand?' she asked, and I flushed as I looked down at the sports bandage I'd wrapped around my wrist that morning, and the rash underneath it immediately started up itching again. It'd somehow got worse overnight, even though I'd taken Maisie's bracelet off. I hadn't wanted to go to the class with it on display, all red and nasty – I wasn't about to inflict that on my sparring partner.

'Nah, not really, it's just a rash,' I said honestly, as we walked over to our bags to get a drink, and she gave me another long look as if I'd said 'Nah, it's just that I think aliens are talking to me through the chip the CIA put in my arm.' I was going to ask what I'd said that was weird, but when I took a swig of water and turned back she was on her way out of the room, bag slung over her back, ponytail bouncing. I blinked after her, worried it was something I'd said or done. Was the girl a sore loser or something?

So much for my zen. I felt vaguely unsettled as Master Yeun led the warm-down. The idea was to stretch out, to give our minds and muscles equal time to relax after the intense workout, but I couldn't seem to settle at all – I found myself constantly shifting my stance, my mind wandering back to the moths, or Dad's disbelief, or Mom's letter ...

At last we stood to attention and bowed again. The lesson was over. Master Yeun came up to me and shook my hand, and I bowed to her.

'Your style is interesting, Miss Helsing,' she said. 'Where did you train before?'

'All over the place,' I said. 'London, San Francisco, Hong Kong ... my family moves around a lot.'

'Ah,' she said, with a smile. She must have seen it in my fighting style, although how, I had no idea. 'That's very interesting. You've certainly earned your brown belt. Are you training for your black belt?'

'I've started,' I said. 'My last teacher said I was about halfway there – there's a lot I haven't covered yet, though.'

'Well, we will definitely work on that if you decide to join us regularly. One piece of advice I would give you: your reactions are good, but your mind is constantly in motion.'

I flushed. Was it that obvious?

'I think you have quite a lot going on in your life right now, don't you?' Master Yeun went on. I nodded dumbly, unexpectedly touched, half afraid I might cry if I tried to speak. 'A black belt needs to be able to face whatever comes with calm and poise, but that doesn't mean pushing away your emotions. Instead, try working with them. Allow them

50

to exist alongside you, and you'll find they won't bother you so much. That is what it really means to be so strong that nothing can disturb the peace in your mind.'

'I'll try to remember,' I choked. 'Thank you.'

I changed back into my tracksuit and T-shirt and stripped the bandage off my wrist to let some air get to the rash, which was burning again now. Then I hurried out of the church, turning her words over and over in my mind. Could I feel everything I was feeling, with everything that was going on, and still be so strong and focused that I could fight like a Master?

I couldn't get my head around it, so I shoved it aside for the moment. I had a much simpler mission to be getting on with.

CHAPTER SEVEN

The market was a vibrant place despite the drizzly weather, each stall covered over with white tarpaulin to keep the goods dry. A lot of the stalls were selling art, or upmarket homewares that would have looked totally in keeping with the Eclectic Modern Weird style of our new house.

Dad had pressed a neatly rolled bundle of crisp Scottish banknotes into my hand as I'd left that morning. Even for him, it was a silly amount of money, and it was burning a hole in my pockets right now.

There were clay bowls and vases, polished antique silver, abstract paintings and second-hand musical instruments. I half expected Julie Andrews to jump out from behind the banjos and sing a song about it. I spent a few conflicted minutes looking longingly at a small, heavy bronze stag that cost half my wardrobe budget, and then turned away and saw the racks of clothes and the sign: 'Gemini Vintage'.

I gave a little audible 'ooh' as I hurried over. The stall was packed with crowded racks of clothes from all sorts of eras. I started to thumb through them, pausing to admire a pretty green beaded flapper dress and a lovely red jacket with a hanging label that read 'Edwardian Ladies' hunting coat'. There was also a little table piled with plastic cups with lids and a pretty handwritten sign: *Free lemonade for window shoppers!* I grinned and picked one up, still thirsty from my workout, and sipped it through a straw while I looked at the racks. It was sour and sweet and delicious.

To my surprise, at the end of the rack there was a collection of furs – black, brown and white. They looked real. I reached out for one, to see if it felt as real as it looked and, as my fingers brushed past the soft hairs and touched the slightly cracked leather underneath, I had the weirdest sensation.

It was a smell, first. I could smell strong perfume and even stronger cigarette smoke. I wanted to look around to see where it was coming from, but it was as if my fingers and my gaze were both glued to the fur, and now I could hear loud laughter . . .

The woman was standing in front of me, black hair slicked down into a perfect curl on her cheek. It was night. It was cold. Her breath misted in the air as she grinned towards me, beckoning, but not for me – her gaze was fixed somewhere over my shoulder. Behind her I could see dancing lights and hear the soft wail of a saxophone.

She was wearing the fur clutched around her shoulders over a thin satin gown. She laughed carelessly, her head thrown back.

My hand dropped from the fabric and I recoiled with a small gasp. The plastic cup slipped from my grasp and bounced on the pavement, and the last few drops of lemonade splashed all over my feet.

OK, that about does it.

I shook the lemonade off my shoes and bent to pick up the cup, my hands shaking.

Either I was definitely for real being haunted, or Edinburgh was swimming in so much psychic energy it was a wonder anyone could get anything done.

Or perhaps I was crazy, after all.

I glanced around at the market, at the bright grey sky and the people strolling about their business, my heart racing. I heard a church bell tolling somewhere nearby and the sound of cars revving on the main street.

I twisted my fingers in front of me, trying not to panic. It didn't exactly seem like anyone else was being bothered by apparitions. But I had *seen* her, the woman, wearing the fur – smelled her smoke, heard the jazz playing in the background!

I dropped the cup into the trash and scraped my hands through my hair. Hallucinations, strange scents ...

I better not be getting a brain tumour. I refuse to have a brain tumour.

But, well. I was facing ... *something*. And I should probably hope it was a ghost, because I'd seen Dad's research – the stuff that didn't get into the books – and I would far rather live with a ghost than brain cancer, or schizophrenia, or any number of other illnesses that could cause this sort of thing. Dad always joked that he should write up his huge file of medical discoveries into a companion book for *OOOOG*, call it *What It Is When It Isn't a Ghost*.

Didn't seem quite so funny right now. In fact, I felt ... well, *sick*.

'All right there?'

I jumped at the sound of a girl's voice: Scottish, and familiar. I turned, and blinked in surprise. It was my tall, blonde ju-jitsu opponent.

'Oh, hi,' I said. 'Sure, I'm ... I'm ...' The word 'fine' hovered on the tip of my tongue, but I couldn't seem to make myself say it. I felt dizzy. Everything suddenly seemed blurry around the edges.

Suddenly something gripped my elbow and I almost threw my arm back in a hard rear elbow strike before I realised that it was the girl – she'd come to my side and taken my arm. I hadn't seen her move.

'Come on, sit,' she was saying.

Yeah, maybe I should do that. I let her steer me to a chair behind the stall table.

'Is this OK?' I muttered, vaguely. 'The stall ...'

'It's fine,' said the girl. 'Here, have some lemonade. Is there someone you want me to call?'

Hello, Mr Helsing? Your daughter's just had a psychic vision and fainted in the middle of New Town. Can you come pick her up?

What's that? You'll come as soon as you've finished writing up this one blog post?

'No,' I said, 'I'm all right. I just had a little ... moment. Maybe I'm dehydrated,' I admitted, and took another sip of my lemonade. 'Sorry,' I added.

'For what,' the girl said shrewdly, 'Kicking my ass in class, or nearly fainting all over my stall?'

'Your stall?' I blinked, and the girl came properly into focus. She was wearing a neat 1940s ensemble with a pencil skirt and white blouse, her hair twisted up away from her face and rolled on top of her head – with her undercut, it was half victory roll, half Mohawk. A necklace with a lotus flower pendant gleamed around her neck. 'Oh!' I said.

'Well, my step-mum's really, but my sister and I work here, and she's out of town with Dad, so basically it's mine all mine.' She laughed and stuck out her hand towards me. We shook again, and this time there was nothing uneasy about her grip. 'I'm Vesta,' she said.

Odd name, I thought, but didn't say. It rang a bell, but

55

I wasn't sure where from. Maybe it was Scottish. 'Diana Helsing,' I said. I stood up, experimentally. No head rush. Sure, there was still the creeping suspicion that something was really wrong ... but that was too big to look at, right now. I smiled at Vesta and tried to focus on something normal. 'You were really good, you know. In class. I thought you had me for a minute there.'

'I totally had you,' Vesta said, waving a hand carelessly, gold and silver plated bangles jangling on her wrist. 'I just let you get the upper hand because you were new. That arm bar was brutal, though, you really nailed it. My elbow's still recovering.' I paused, trying to unpack whether she was kidding. She was grinning, but I kinda suspected that was her default facial expression.

'I ... uh ... I saw you leave early,' I said. 'That wasn't – I mean, I didn't do anything ...'

'What, did I bail on the warm-down because you'd bested me in single combat? No! I had to come get changed and help Minnie set out the stall so that people could come and collapse all over my furs.'

I flushed again, but then a softer girl's voice said, 'V, are you teasing the customers again?' A tall green velvet curtain at the back of the stall parted to reveal ... Vesta. Or that was what my brain tried to tell me for a second before it caught up with the rest of me and said, *Oh. Twins!*

They weren't actually a hundred per cent identical – the second one's face was a little rounder, and she was closer to my height. Her hair was the same colour and the same thick, wavy texture, but she was wearing it loose and hanging down over her shoulders in waves. She was also wearing a crown of plastic daisies, a pendant with a lightning bolt, and a long, flowing dress covered with prints of sunflowers.

'Don't let V's bravado fool you,' the girl – who had to be

Minnie – said, hanging up a stunning 1930s wedding dress studded with pearls and a fantastically ugly 1970s pant suit in yellow corduroy. 'She puts her stockings on one foot at a time, just like the rest of us.'

She came to stand beside her sister, across a table piled with faded T-shirts from where I was standing.

There was something hypnotic about the two of them, stood side by side. It was partly the twin thing, and the clothes – the effect was distinctly bizarre, as if they were a single time traveller, meeting themselves on the way home from World War Two and Woodstock.

But . . . it wasn't just the clothes. In fact, I realised it wasn't the girls at all, it was a physical sensation. I could hear my heartbeat slow and strong in my ears, blocking out the noise from the rest of the market and the street beyond.

But weirdly, unlike the low-level panic or the hallucinations or the dreaming, this wasn't an unpleasant feeling. Not at all. In fact, I felt the tension leave my shoulders and my neck, just seep away. I felt *good*.

Minnie gave Vesta a sideways glance and then moved around the table, and the feeling abruptly stopped.

All right, better. Feels . . . normal.

'You all right, Diana?' Vesta asked. 'You were shivering. You sure we can't call someone? Or maybe interest you in a lovely cashmere cardie?'

The sight of my clothes in pieces all over the attic room flooded back to me, and I remembered why I'd been fondling the furs in the first place. I probably ought to have excused myself and gone home to lie down in a dark room and pray I wasn't dying, but if I did that, I'd only have to come out again tomorrow, and in the same tracksuit bottoms.

My overtired brain made a decision for me.

'I had a bit of a wardrobe disaster, in the move,' I heard

myself saying. 'Actually, more of a wardrobe apocalypse. I pretty much need a whole new one.'

'Well, I think you'd look lovely in this,' Minnie said, fishing out one of the cardigans. She was right, it was pretty nice – cute lemon-yellow with a flowery design in cream beads along the neckline and down the sleeves. 'So, you're a Diana? You didn't say she was a Diana,' Minnie went on, glaring accusingly at Vesta as she held up the cardigan against my shoulders. Vesta stuck her tongue out at Minnie. 'You're a Roman goddess!'

'I ... well, named after one, yeah,' I said. 'If people *want* to worship me I try not to object ...'

'We're goddesses too. I mean, named for them, obviously. I'm Minerva, except to my sister,' she added.

Vesta rolled her eyes. 'I'm sorry about Minnie. She's a nerd.'

'No, it's cool! That is,' I added, grinning sheepishly, 'I'm kind of a nerd about names too. Diana, the huntress. It's awesome. I'm totally obsessed with all that stuff, stags and foxes – well, and Wonder Woman. What is it, Minerva for wisdom and Vesta for ... er ...' I trailed off, trying to think.

'Protective fire,' said Vesta firmly. 'Defence of hearth and home.' She paused. 'And virgins,' she added glumly, but when I blinked at her, uncertain how to reply to that, she laughed. 'No, I don't know what our parents were thinking either. No wonder I took up punching people as a hobby.'

Minerva sniggered and handed me the cardigan to try on. I pulled off my coat and shrugged it on. It fitted pretty well. I smoothed it down ...

A strong breeze ... the scent of flowers, and the sea ...

It was brief, this time, oddly familiar but not so strong. A split second of blossom and salt, and then I was back in the market, with the twin goddesses, and the Sunday lunch-time shoppers strolling by. I peeled it off again carefully and, as I did, I saw the label – Made in Hong Kong, 1948 – and I knew where I had smelled that flower scent before. Orchid trees, growing by the shore.

'That looks painful,' said, Minerva, pulling an 'ouch' face and dragging me fully back to the real world. I didn't know what she meant for a moment, before she nodded at the exposed rash on my wrist.

I hesitated, vaguely embarrassed, but the twins seemed more concerned than disgusted, so I just sighed. 'You know what, I don't know what to do with it. It keeps itching. I thought I might have been allergic to a cheap bracelet I got for my birthday, but it hasn't got any better since I took it off, and that was yesterday.'

'When was your birthday?' Minerva said faintly. She glanced at Vesta, then back at me. 'You weren't sixteen, were you?'

'Yeah. On Friday.'

'Us too!' said Vesta. I stared at her, genuinely not understanding what she'd said for a good couple of seconds.

'What? No, that's too weird.' I stared at them. 'You're playing *let's see what we can make the gullible American believe*, right?' I folded my arms. 'I am so on to you.'

The twins exchanged wary glances, and I got the impression they were having a whole conversation based on the micro-expressions that only twins could read. Then Vesta's grin bounced back, brighter than ever.

'OK, you got us,' she laughed. 'Our birthday's not for another few days. We were born on the Summer Solstice, so it's like the whole city's throwing us a big party. Are you going?'

'Well ... sorta,' I said. 'I'm going to a book launch.'

'Wow!' said Minerva.

'Not really. The author is my dad. Attendance is compulsory. There won't be anyone I know there and, trust me, the book isn't that interesting. I'd much rather come to the Solstice festival.' *Ideally with a certain hot young man I met on a train and will probably never see again*, I thought, trying not to sigh.

'Hey, maybe you can explore a little after the party,' said Minerva. 'We might even run into each other.'

They gave each other another Look that I couldn't translate, and I turned back to the racks. I was actually really starting to like these two – weird as they were. But I couldn't think too hard about meeting them at the Solstice.

I wasn't even convinced I'd still be walking around come Friday night.

The twins eventually waved me off down the street laden down with bags – shirts, dresses, and that Edwardian hunting jacket, too. I clutched them tight, as if they were somehow magical clothes that could banish a ghost or cure a tumour.

I had to go home. I had to talk to my dad.

CHAPTER EIGHT

'And so, as that Witch Doctor told me in Tower Hamlets: if you want to wear the shoes, you have to eat the broccoli!'

Edinburgh Central Library rang with laughter and applause as Dad raised his glass one last time, tilted it in appreciation and stepped away from the central table piled high with copies of *OOOOG*. I grinned and clapped too, even though I'd heard the joke several dozen times at various events. If the hauntings ever dried up, Dad would have a pretty good chance at making a living as a stand-up comedian.

The crowd dispersed, mingling among the bookshelves, clutching plastic cups of white wine and red velvet cupcakes. The publishing types in their little black dresses mixed and chatted with the fans – mainly goths and hippies in long black coats and heavy silver jewellery.

I wasn't really feeling the urge to socialise and, thank God, nobody seemed to be about to make me.

I hadn't mentioned the hallucinations to Dad.

I skulked by the graphic novels, reading the spines,

wanting to pull out the latest Wonder Woman and go hide in a corner somewhere. But my hands were full. How were you supposed to eat a cupcake while holding a drink, anyway? Not with dignity, that was for sure.

From a high window nearby, I could hear the *thump-thump* of loud music and the rumble of a much larger, rowdier crowd than the one that'd turned out for the book launch. The Summer Solstice Festival was in full swing down on Grassmarket.

I wondered if Vesta and Minerva and Alex were there right now ...

'Hi, Diana!' I looked around to see who'd spoken to me. It was a girl, maybe fourteen, tall and red-headed and beaming with barely controlled fannish glee. She was wearing a freakishly convincing rabbit mask pushed up on top of her head.

'Hello,' I said, awkwardly trying to tear my eyes from the floppy latex ears hanging down on the sides of her face.

She had to be a Helsingite. It was a cute nickname, and, hey, I thought it was great that Dad had fans. I just didn't love interacting with them.

'Have you seen the head?' the girl asked. 'The one at the museum?'

'No,' I said. I was drawing breath to engage, to tell her I thought I'd sit this one out because – you know, severed heads, no thank you – but she rolled right on, her voice going squeaky with excitement.

'Oh, you should, it's amazing! Genuine seventeenth-century woman's severed head! Where did it come from? Who was she?'

I smiled blankly and shrugged.

'They had staff doing bag searches,' the girl went on. 'The back doors were alarmed. The CCTV was working, but nobody's seen it yet – has Jake asked? Are they going to let him look? There won't be anything there,' she added, without pausing for an answer or apparently to draw breath. 'There is no way that anyone could have brought that head into the building and put it down by the Maiden without someone seeing, and yet nobody saw a thing! Isn't it exciting?'

'It's pretty horrible,' I said.

'So exciting!' the girl said again, as if we were agreeing.

I glanced around for some way out of this conversation, but I couldn't see any escape, unless I wanted to fake knowing someone, or tell her I needed to talk to Dad. A very flawed plan: I would probably actually have to talk to Dad.

Then, I noticed that the girl was clutching a red Sharpie and a dog-eared paperback copy of *Death in Hollywood*, one of Dad's first bestsellers. It was the first one where I'd turned up as a supporting character. At twelve years old, I'd exposed the 'haunted' motel's owner for a fraud – that is, instead of running screaming from his fake ghost I had turned my ju-jitsu white belt skills on him, beating his very corporeal ass with a Gideon Bible.

The memory made me smile. No severed heads there, or weird visions. I glanced over at Dad, feeling the urge to share, but he was listening intently to a middle-aged lady in a knitted purple poncho and pentagram earrings.

'You want me to sign it?' I asked, turning back to the girl, hoping to get her off the subject of the museum. She nodded, her face lighting up. 'Also, what's with the mask?'

'They're selling them down at the festival,' the girl said, and I felt another strange pang of jealousy. It'd be so great to buy a mask and slip into the crowd and dance my worries away ... 'Anyway,' she went on, 'the thing you have to consider is: why would a woman in the seventeenth century have been beheaded?'

I sighed, accepting that this was the topic we were going to stay with, and waited for her to answer her own question – after living with Dad for sixteen years, I could spot a rhetorical device a mile off – though I couldn't help raking through the little British history I'd absorbed in the last couple of years. The 1600s: English Civil War, religious nutbags on all points of the Christian spectrum beating the crap out of each other ...

'I'm guessing they were killed for *being women*, half the time,' I muttered. 'Oh – you mean witchcraft.'

'The Maiden was used to execute loads of Scottish witches in the seventeenth century. There was a huge panic. People just didn't understand that witches are *good*, you know? They were threatened by their connection to the earth.'

I think they were mostly threatened by their uteruses, I thought, but I let the point go – it was never, ever a good idea to talk paganism with a Helsingite. Whether they were for or against, if you didn't want to hear about it at length, you had to learn not to ask.

'The question is, if this woman was genuinely a witch, is it her spirit that's come back to haunt the thing that killed her, or is someone or some*thing* else doing this? Or maybe she was just a normal woman – of course *real* witches wouldn't have been caught, unless they were like Isobel Gowdie – she survived burning, you know, *and* hanging! This woman might have been a healer, or a horse-whisperer ... what do you think, Diana?'

I think I want out of here.

I took a breath, tempted to have an opinion, but knowing that if I did I could be here arguing it for hours.

But at that moment Dad clapped his hands for attention.

'Thank you all so much for coming,' he said. 'We have to leave the lovely librarians to close up now, but if you want to follow along, we'll be reassembling in a pub just around the corner.'

Great excuse. Thank you, Dad!

I gave the girl an apologetic smile. 'Gotta go! I'm going to the pub to help set up. Thanks for coming.'

'Oh, OK. It was so great to meet you!' The girl beamed at me, and I felt a tiny bit guilty as I slipped out of the room, leaving Dad to be carried after me on a cloud of admiration and leather jackets, and headed down the road towards the pub alone. Maybe I could grab a couple of minutes to myself before I had to face the after-party.

As I walked slowly down the steep and curving road towards Grassmarket, the festival atmosphere rose all around me: the thumping of the music, the smells of hot dogs and spilled beer. People flooded past, almost all of them wearing animal masks just like the one the Helsingite girl had. There were rabbits, foxes, owls and stags, wolves and weasels, and more.

'Hurry up,' one of a group of women in crow masks called out, and the others tilted their beaks towards her in eerie unison.

I was watching them, instead of watching my step, and I stumbled over my feet. I yelped, and grabbed the closest thing to stop my fall, which turned out to be the warm, solid arms of a guy in a blue shirt and black jeans. I looked up, flushing, into the face of a stag mask, with stiff latex antlers that swept back from its long face.

'God, sorry,' I said.

The stag held on to my elbows, steadying me. 'Sorry, I didn't – *Diana*?'

I knew that voice. I looked up, and the eyes behind the mask's empty sockets were piercing and blue.

'Alex?'

He reached up and tugged off the mask. It was him.

'Diana, this is incredible – I couldn't believe I'd walked off without getting your number,' he blurted out.

'I *know*,' I said, and a layer of anxiety I hadn't even realised I'd been carrying around lifted off my shoulders. It really was a mistake. He hadn't left without my number on purpose. Of course not! 'How dumb are we?'

'So dumb,' Alex laughed. We were still holding on to each other's arms, taking up half the pavement like giant dorks, but I was damned if I was going to be the first one to pull away. 'Well, um, look – are you going to the Festival? Are you meeting someone?'

'I ...' I was so good, I hesitated for a full five seconds, which is a long time when there's a boy like Alex waiting for your answer. 'Nope. I'm just here for the music and the freaky masks,' I said.

I could text Dad in a minute. He wouldn't mind me bailing on his after-party, I was certain – it wasn't as if he was usually strict about where I went or who with. He probably wouldn't even notice I was gone.

'You want to go get a drink?' Alex asked. He finally dropped my elbows, and I tried not to feel too bereft.

Don't get carried away, Di. He's still just some boy.

We descended the hill on to Grassmarket, and into what seemed like a totally different world. Down here, the music throbbed in time to the beat of my heart, on top of a base rumble of muffled laughter and chatter from the masked crowd that thronged over the pavement and spilled into the road. Coloured flags with blazing suns on them hung from the street lamps. The smell of whisky and smoke and burger vans wafted over the heads of the crowd.

'We have to get you a mask,' Alex said, pointing to a stall festooned with animal heads. We strolled over and I scanned

66

the racks. There was another stag, but matching Alex would probably be creepy, and I couldn't shout down the little nerd in my mind who insisted stags were male and it'd look weird.

'I'll take a wolf,' I told the lady standing by the till. I handed over £15 in fresh-minted Scottish notes and tugged the mask down over my face, trying to tuck my hair in underneath. 'What do you think?' I said, turning to Alex.

'Hot,' Alex dead-panned, nodding approvingly.

I laughed, thankful that he couldn't see how hard I was blushing. I bit back a comment about chasing him down and devouring him. It was going well so far, but there was still plenty of time for me to make this awkward.

We wandered between the stalls for a while, sipping little plastic glasses of spiced whisky that made my eyes water, perusing the pagan-ish Solstice gifts – heavy on the *ish*, but whatever works. Bundles of twigs, plastic flower crowns, thin white Druid capes, dangly pentagrams and strings of beads fought for space with the ubiquitous neon glowsticks.

Out of nowhere, a blast of flame went up from my left, and I gasped and twisted around.

'Hey look, what did I tell you about fire-eaters?' Alex said.

We hurried over and found a crowd gathered around a shirtless man with black hair so long it had to be a health and safety issue. He raised a torch to his face and blew out a fireball that made both of us cringe back half a step. Then he lit the ends of two flaming batons and started to twirl them back and forth, drawing stinging orange after-images in the air, swinging his hair and his hips in time to the music like an incredibly metal cheer captain.

'Fire-eater selfie?' I suggested, and Alex grinned and leaned in close to my shoulder so I could capture us both, and the glowing trail of the fire-eater's batons, in the frame. We took one with masks, and one without, and then Alex went to get us some snacks so I swiftly sent them both to Instagram, tagging Maisie. Barely ten seconds later, my phone buzzed with a private message:

Lord have mercy. Do him, Diana. Do him for all of us.

I will make that noble sacrifice

I wrote back, and then put my phone away, feeling guilty.

'So, how have you found Edinburgh?' Alex asked, coming back with two mini haggis burgers in paper cups.

I hesitated for a second. Truthfully? I'd found it disorientating and creepy. I wasn't about to explain why, though. I was very happy in my little bubble here, playing at not being weird. 'I kinda love it,' I told him. 'Like, did you even know how pretty it is here?'

Alex laughed. 'I had noticed. But it's always nice when an outsider says it.'

We settled into the awkward rhythm of a first date – chit-chat about Edinburgh, about life, shows we were addicted to, books and music we had to share some time. Our tastes turned out to be wildly different, but to his credit he seemed open to the idea that Wonder Woman was the greatest superhero of all time, and in return I was willing to promise I would listen, like *really* listen, to some Blind Lemon Jefferson.

All of a sudden, while we were watching a procession of Druid-types in long robes waving sticks around in a semi-meaningful manner, I felt a presence at my elbow – the sensation of someone hovering nearby. I glanced around, realising with a guilty lurch that I hadn't texted Dad yet ...

'Hey, Diana!' said Vesta. 'How are you doing?'

'Oh, hey, guys.' I grinned, lifting my mask. 'How'd you know it was me?'

68

They weren't dressed like full-on time-travellers any more: Vesta was wearing black jeans, a black T-shirt and a grey trench coat that looked like it might have been army surplus a hundred years ago. Minerva was in a leather jacket and a dress with foxes on it, but she had a magnificent 1920s mosaic comb in her hair. I noticed they were both still wearing the charms they'd had on before, the lotus flower and the lightning bolt.

'Pretty sure we've only sold one red Edwardian ladies' hunting jacket this year,' Vesta said. 'It really does suit you, by the way. Very chic with the jeans.'

I smiled and flushed at the compliment, and compulsively smoothed down the stiff vintage fabric. 'I *love* it.'

'Nice to see you again,' Minerva said. 'Are you enjoying the Festival?'

'Very much,' I said, casting a shy grin at Alex. 'Alex, this is Vesta and Minerva, they run a vintage stall in New Town. This is Alex.'

'I'm her date,' Alex said, taking my arm. Something inside of me melted like ice cream on a hot day. I probably blushed – more dignified than what I wanted to do, which was point and grin and say, *Do you see what's happening to me right now? I'm on a date with* those cheekbones.

'So, how are you doing? Are you coming to class tomorrow?' Vesta said, raising her voice slightly over the sound of the Druids behind us smacking their twig bundles together and declaiming something about death.

'Yeah, definitely!'

'Good, because I want a rematch. Oh hey, how's the wrist?'

'It's ... fine,' I said, even though it'd been a week and the itching hadn't let up much. I wasn't about to say that in front of Alex.

'And how was the book launch?'

'Oh yeah, it was good ...' I realised that I hadn't actually mentioned the launch, or Dad's work, to Alex at all.

Holy awkward moment, Batman.

I stared at Minerva, hoping that she was a little less clueless than her sister, or that she could read my mind, or at least translate from the twitching of my eyebrows. *Guys! It's nice to see you too, but you heard him say we're on a date, right?* I let my eyes flicker from Minerva to Alex and back again. *DATE.*

'Well,' Alex said suddenly, 'we're away for a dance, so ...' He took my hand. His skin was warm and soft and I suppressed a shudder of delight.

'Oh sure, off you go, have a great time, you two! I'm sure we'll run into you again in a bit,' Vesta said.

I couldn't help frowning back at her over my shoulder as Alex led me through the crowd. I swear, her tone was so insanely bright and cheery she was starting to give me weird Stepford vibes, as if she'd been replaced with a robot programmed to find everything I did adorable.

My mind didn't linger on the twins too long, though. How could it, when Alex's thumb was soft and warm on the curve of my wrist, his pulse lightly beating over mine?

CHAPTER NINE

When we'd left the twins and the Druids behind, he stopped and looked down at me with a half-apologetic smile. 'Sorry if they were your friends – I just want you all to myself, is that terrible?'

'No, but I think that line may have been,' I said, arching an eyebrow at him. 'Anyway, where's this dance I was promised?'

His eyes lit up, glinting in the light of another flare of yellow from the fire-eaters. The crowd went *ooh*. I felt the same.

'I know just the place.' He grinned, and then he leaned down and gave me a kiss on my left cheek, barely more than a brush of stubbly skin and warmth.

I floated a couple of inches off the ground as I followed him. We crossed the road, and headed away from the stage and the stalls, back the way we'd arrived, except instead of climbing the spiralling hill, we headed down a street that seemed to loom in over us, dark bricks of hugely tall buildings blocking out the sky, so the last dregs of sunset were replaced with grimy street-lamp orange.

The crowd thinned, though there were still plenty of people spilling out of the bars and staggering along the road. We skirted a gang of foxes and owls drunkenly hanging on to each other's shoulders as we passed underneath a huge bridge.

'Here,' said Alex, nodding towards what looked, to be honest, like a complete dive of a bar. 'They have the best folk-goth fusion in here,' he said. When I gave him a sceptical look, he chuckled and squeezed my hand. 'You'll see. C'mon.'

We stepped inside and immediately descended a steep and sticky flight of stairs. A thumping, rhythmic bass drifted up from below. The place smelled of smoke and alcohol and sweat. At the bottom, Alex pushed open a heavy door and I stepped through into a hot, dark space with low vaulted ceilings, crowded with dancing figures shadowed against flashing lights.

It was, like he'd said, essentially folk music. But not like any folk music I'd ever heard before. It was heavy on the bass and drums, as well as the cacophony of fiddles and flutes and, yep, actual bagpipes laying down a drone like the death throes of a monstrous creature.

The scattered animal masks in the crowd cast much spookier shadows down here in the dark, horns and pointed ears mixed in with flying hair and laughing faces lit up in flashes of red and blue. The crowd jigged and swayed to the music as Alex led me along one side of the room. Some of them were just moshing on the spot, but there were also groups of people on the dance floor weaving in and out of each other's arms in a complex pattern, twisting on the spot, changing direction – and all without a single instruction from the musicians.

'Do you all just *know* that stuff?' I had to raise my voice over the bagpipes and the stamping of feet.

'Eh, I had to do it at school, it sort of sticks in the brain after you've done it a couple of million times.' Alex grinned. 'Want to try it?'

He didn't wait for my answer – which would've been a mildly intimidated yes – before leading me into the swaying, sweating crowd of dancers.

Alex linked his arm in mine and suddenly we were off, prancing and spinning around in twisting circles, squishing in with the people on either side of us and then backing away again like flower petals opening and closing. Alex kept up a steady stream of instructions in my ear whenever it wasn't obvious. 'Round this way ... now back that way ... go on, follow that woman!'

We formed an arch and, one by one, the other dancers threaded through our hands. I laughed and gasped, and by the time the song scratched to a halt I found myself leaning against Alex to catch my breath.

I realised, but far too late to give a damn, that we were suddenly closer than I'd usually go for on a first date. My hand was flat against his chest. I could feel its warmth through his shirt.

He said something, but I didn't catch it.

'Huh?'

He leaned down to speak into my ear. His breath was warm and I could feel his smile.

'There's somewhere a bit quieter if you want a sit down,' he said.

I didn't *need* to stop – it was heavy going, this goth folk stuff, but it wasn't like a full ju-jitsu session or anything. On the other hand, the way I was feeling right now, the way he was looking at me ... yes, a sit down sounded good.

We made our way out of the crowd, ducking to avoid the flailing arms of the dancers as the band struck up another song. Alex led the way over to the far wall, pushed open a door, and I found myself descending stone steps into a small, dark hallway with bare brick walls and a single dim light bulb overhead.

'Hey, are you sure it's down here?' I said. 'This doesn't look very public.'

'Hah, you're right, it looks pretty dodgy! That's just the aesthetic,' Alex said. 'The chill-out room's just down here.'

I felt a twist of unease, deep in my stomach. And then I ignored it. I was second-guessing him.

Trust your instincts, remember?

I'd learned that the hard way. That same flicker of unease had been there the first time I'd met Skeevy Steve, and I'd ignored it because he was hot and he seemed to like me, and sure enough he had turned out to be a cheating scumbag.

I was second-guessing myself. Alex was a good guy, everything had told me so – up until right now. Also, I was quite prepared to beat his ass into a pulp if he turned out to be a serial killer.

Satisfied with my logic, I held on to Alex's hand and followed him a little further down the hall and around a corner and down another flight of grotty concrete steps. The ceilings suddenly seemed to get very high, and one wall turned from brick to old damp stone, like the outside of a run-down old church. The hallway in front of me seemed to extend into the darkness.

OK, this actually wasn't right.

'Alex, come on,' I said, stopping at the bottom of the steps, letting go of his hand to cross my arms. 'I'm trusting you, but I'm not a complete moron. Where are we going? I don't think we're even in the same building any more.'

'Er ...' Alex scratched the back of his head. 'I really thought it was down here.'

'Really?' I arched an eyebrow at him and he shrugged. 'Were you seriously going to go off down the pitch black – this isn't even a corridor, dude, I think this is an alleyway! – rather than admit you were going the wrong way?'

Alex had the decency to look sheepish. It was hot. I probably didn't need to keep thinking that – when I found an expression on his face that *wasn't* hot, I would be sure to make a note.

'Sorry,' he said. He took my hands. 'We'll go back.'

But he didn't move.

'You have to admit, though ...' His thumb ran over the back of my hand and I tried to breathe evenly. 'It's kinda nice to be alone like this.'

'Sure,' I said. My voice came out breathy and deep.

'Can I ...?'

I grinned. He leaned in. I let my shoulders rest against the cool stone wall and brought up my hand to cup the back of his neck.

I've had more romantic kisses. But for sheer knee-buckling, brain-melting intensity, Alex's kiss took the gold and then ran a breathless victory lap. His hand was on the wall beside my head, and our bodies were pressed close.

We pulled apart, and I looked up at him.

A wholly different kind of shudder ran down my back.

CHAPTER TEN

There was a cold nothing behind his eyes. He looked up and stared at something over the top of my head – but there was nothing there, nothing but solid stone wall.

'I have her.' Mechanically, still not meeting my eyes, his free hand grabbed my shoulder.

I reached up to grab it, to twist his wrist and throw him down. It should have been easy. But when I tried to push off from the wall, my hands found only empty air. My stomach dropped into my boots as I lost my balance and Alex pushed me back, *through* where the wall had been.

It was like falling through a column of freezing air. I saw his face, expressionless and implacable as a stone, then a chilling blast forced my eyes shut, darkness closed over my head and the world turned around me.

I landed on my side on a cold floor in pitch blackness. I gasped and pushed myself up, my hands stinging from the impact. Hot, acid panic rose up and burned the back of my throat as I scrambled to my feet. I fumbled behind me and found the wall, solid stone – as solid as it had been before my date shoved me through it.

'Alex.' I spoke through gritted teeth, not really expecting a reply.

His face, right before he'd pushed me ... it had seemed *empty*, as if all the life that'd been there a second earlier, all the passion that was in his kiss, had just been drained out of him. *I have her*, he'd said.

Who was he talking to?

The darkness was absolute, cold ... and familiar.

The squeaking of the moths didn't come as a surprise. Their harsh *skree* was quiet at first, growing louder, coming *closer*.

But I was awake.

I was truly, horribly awake, alone in the dark, cut off from escape. This was *real*.

There was a sound like a thousand wings beating together, and then ... silence. All I could hear was my own fast breathing, the scratching of my fingers on stone as I tried to find the hidden mechanism that would *let me out, for God's sake, let me out ...*

And then I realised there was another sound, close, almost inaudible under my choked breath.

Something else in here was breathing too.

I swallowed, pressed my back flat to the stone and raised my fists.

'This is your only warning!' I yelled. My voice echoed. 'Come any closer and I'll break your face.'

'*Fleming.*'

The voice sounded like cold marshes.

'I know it's you, Fleming. You've come back to me, after all this time ...'

Fleming.

Like as in *Kara* Fleming? My fists sagged a little.

Mom, what did you do?

'And now,' the horrible voice whispered, 'I—'

Something grabbed my shoulders and I screamed as I was dragged back, held tight in real, strong arms.

The dim alley was like midday after the pitch black of … of wherever the hell I just was, and for a split second I stared stupidly, taking in details, unable to understand what I was seeing.

The arms that held me were clothed in stiff grey fabric. The nails were painted neon blue and slightly chipped.

Alex's head was buried in the wall, up to his shoulders. The supposedly solid stone rippled and flowed around him – every last rational brain cell in my head tried to tell me that wasn't what I was seeing, but, deeper down, I knew it made perfect sense. If someone tried to drive my head into a wall and I could make it insubstantial, I would …

A blonde girl in a leather jacket was holding him there, her fists balled in the back of his shirt.

'Got her,' Vesta gasped behind my ear. 'Do it, Min!'

Minerva heaved Alex forward. He tried to kick back at her as he fell through the wall, but she deftly hopped out of the way. The wall swallowed him up and closed behind him.

'Go!' Minerva said.

Vesta let go of my shoulders and grabbed my hand and then we were running, my stumbling feet pounding up the concrete steps. Her shoulder struck the wall and her trench coat flapped at my shins as we took the corner but she didn't slow down. I was dragged along behind, under the exposed light bulb, through another metal door. I didn't know where we were going, but away was good enough for me.

We burst out of the dingy corridor and into the club, the darkness and the flashing lights and the spinning, animalistic crowd. Vesta barely seemed to miss a beat before she pulled me into the middle of the dancers. She snatched the wolf mask off the top of my head.

'Oi!' I heard a voice and twitched around to look. Minerva had caught up and grabbed a crow mask from one of the dancers and thrust my wolf mask into his hand.

'Suits you better,' she said, and dodged out of the way as the man tried to swat her with the mask.

'Coat off,' Vespa ordered. I didn't think, I just obeyed, peeling off the red jacket. She took it from me and bundled it under her coat. Minerva handed me the crow mask and I pulled it on, and then we were running again, heading for the door. By the time we climbed the steep, sticky stairs and burst out into the cool air of the surface world, Minerva was wearing a mouse mask and Vesta a red fox. Vesta dropped my hand and took off running. I made to follow her, but Minerva grabbed my arm and steered me in the opposite direction at a painfully gentle stroll.

'Walk, don't run,' she said, bending her head close to mine. 'Try to blend in, and don't look back. We don't know how many spies he has or how close they're watching you. The masks will help. We'll be out of here soon, try not to panic.'

'What the *hell* is going on here?' I hissed. I felt my throat close over the words.

Minerva squeezed my arm. 'It's all right,' she said. 'V's going to get us a cab and meet us up on the bridge, and then we're going to take you somewhere safe.'

'You didn't answer the question.'

'We will. But not here. There's too much.'

We ambled, leaning on each other, back up the hill to the road outside the Central Library, and stopped on the bridge. I looked over the concrete railing. We were right above the bar where Alex had taken me. I felt sick.

'How did you know?' I stared at her, at her green eyes wary and serious behind the mouse mask. 'How did you know I was down there?'

'We were following you. It's OK,' Minerva said, gently turning my shoulders away from the drop down to the crowded pavement below. 'V will be here soon. He won't follow us up here – too many people. And if he sends his puppet after us, we can throw him off the bridge.'

I leaned on the stone bridge railing. *He* ... the voice in the dark? Then, Alex was *his puppet*?

'Minerva, what ... is he? What exactly did I just go on a date with?'

Minerva just shook her head.

Cabs passed us, just infrequently enough that I twitched to attention at the sight of each one. Just as I was starting to wonder if this was some new kind of trick, if I was wrong to trust the twins, one of them slowed and stopped in front of us. Vesta threw open the rear door and I hesitated, contemplating making a run for it – but then I would be alone, and they'd promised me answers. Minerva gently steered me into the back seat and I didn't resist her.

'You can take that off now,' Vesta murmured, and I peeled off the crow mask and took a deep breath of cool, stale taxicab air.

Minerva gave the driver an address I didn't really catch, and we took off at what felt like a law-defying speed. I stared at Vesta, and she gave me an apologetic smile and squeezed my shoulder.

'Feeling OK?' she asked. 'In ... general terms?' she added, throwing a meaningful glance at the driver.

I blew out a long breath and let my hair dangle over my face. 'I think so. Who the hell even knows,' I said.

I don't normally get car sick, but there was something

about the way the cab swerved around the winding streets and the yellow street lamps cast shifting shadows over the seats that had me bracing myself against the door handle and praying that the ride would be over soon. Bile stung my throat. I had to be on the comedown from a pretty stunning adrenaline spike. It didn't help to know that.

Finally, we pulled up on a street of Georgian houses, like mine, but smaller, decaying and shabby. I clambered out of the taxi as soon as it'd come to a halt and staggered to the sidewalk. My hands found the iron railing and I held on as if the world might tip up and try to throw me off. Minerva paid the driver, and we waited there until the cab had peeled away.

'Where are we?' I asked.

'This is Aunt Isobel's house,' Minerva said, climbing the steps to the front door of a house with dirty windows and cracked brickwork. 'She can help you, I promise.'

She opened the door and I followed her inside. The hallway was dark and cool, a faint light spilling down the stairs, cracked tiles tilting uneasily underfoot. My eyes adjusted to the gloom and, in the shadows, I saw a pair of beady black eyes above a cruel curved beak looking down at me. I froze, swallowing a yelp. There were other things too, furry things, things with pointed ears and long claws ...

Then Vesta flicked on a light switch, and I found myself eye-to-eye with an angry-looking but perfectly immobile vulture.

'Don't mind the taxidermy,' Minerva said, entirely too late. The hallway was lined with animals – there were squirrels, birds, two cats, a duck, and even a large wolf, with eyes that were slightly too bright and bodies that were entirely too still. The vulture was perched on the wooden bannister at the bottom of the stairs, tied on with wire.

I breathed out again, strangely reassured that yes, what I was looking at was thoroughly creepy.

'Girls?' A voice rang out from upstairs, and a silhouette of a woman appeared at the top of the stairs. She stepped forward into the circle of light from the bulb in the hall.

She was very old – at least eighty, at a guess – and her face was a mass of wrinkles, but she stood straight-backed, her hands and feet held like a dancer or a gymnast. She had long white hair in a thick braid that hung over her shoulder, and she was staring at me with a drawn, almost haughty expression.

Out of the corner of my eye, I realised that Vesta and Minerva had stiffened slightly.

'Is this her?' the old lady said. 'Is this truly Kara's daughter?'

CHAPTER ELEVEN

My jaw dropped.

'It's her,' Vesta said.

Isobel descended the stairs, stepping lightly, surprisingly agile for such an old lady. 'Come into the light, dear, let me look at you.'

'You knew my mom?' I blurted, not moving.

Isobel tilted her head, staring at me with eyes like bright green gems. 'Oh yes. This is Kara's daughter.' She smiled, and her face softened with it. She threw her arms around me and gave me a long, warm hug. 'Amazing. After all these years. It's lovely to meet you, dear. Please, come in. You must be wondering what on earth is going on.'

'Yeah, just a bit!' I said as she pulled away. 'I mean, I have these dreams, and then I get here and the moths are just *there* in my room, and then I touch the clothes on the stall and I get this like … this like *psychic vision* or something, and I'm half convinced I'm nuts at this point, and then I meet this boy and he seems really great and I trust him, you know?' I was almost yelling, but I couldn't seem to stop. 'I *trust* him, except in the middle of our first kiss he shoves me through some kind of secret door and I can hear the moths and someone calls me by my mother's name and, yeah, I would have to say I'm wondering, yes!'

Isobel gripped both my hands in hers. 'Oh, my poor child. Follow me, please.'

She beckoned us to follow her along the hall. I didn't move at first, but then Vesta linked her arm in mine.

'C'mon. You don't want to stand in the hall all night, right?'

She had a point.

I let them lead me past the taxidermied animals, past a door into a room where a giant black bear loomed over a sofa, and down a flight of steps into the basement. The stairs were cold and damp smelling. At the bottom, I found myself in a room much like the one in my house where Dad had set up his study. It was fairly well lit by lamps draped in coloured scarves, and there were two comfortable-looking couches upholstered in fraying tapestry covers. Part of the Georgian kitchen was still in place, and several large bookshelves stood along one wall – almost all the spines of the books were old cracked leather, or missing altogether.

'There, now,' said Isobel. 'Sit down and the girls will get you a cup of tea.'

I cast a horrified glance at the three-hundred-year-old kitchen mouldering in the corner – copper and iron rusting away, wood rotting and paint peeling – before I noticed that there was a modern kettle and a stack of chipped teacups on a side table.

Vesta slumped down on one of the couches, which creaked underneath her. 'Not it,' she said.

Minerva rolled her eyes and shrugged off her jacket. She hung it over the head of a taxidermy owl, which she gave a little pat as if to thank it for acting as a coat hook, and then went to boil the kettle.

'Vesta, show Diana the painting,' Isobel said, a little pointedly.

'Ooh, right! Come and see, Diana.' Vesta hopped up from the couch and pulled down one of the thick books from the shelf. It was bound in faded red cloth. I went over to join her, slowly.

'What painting? What's this got to do with anything?'

'It has to do with the three of us,' Minerva said.

Somewhat reluctantly, uncertain just how much more mystery I could take before I threw a foot-stamping toddler tantrum, I looked over Vesta's shoulder.

'It's by this obscure artist from the Hebrides who claimed to be painting what God showed him, back in the 1850s.' She opened the book to a page that had been bookmarked with a shoelace.

I looked down at the painting, and then cast her a sharp look.

The painting was a classical scene – bright blue sky, Doric columns, three young women wearing flowing white togas that magically covered everything that needed to be covered and not much else. Except that behind the women, there was a . . . a *thing*.

'What the—' I bit off the rest of the sentence, not sure how much I ought to be swearing in front of the twins' ancient Aunt Isobel.

It looked like the kind of thing Picasso would have a nightmare about after drinking a whole bottle of absinthe. It was a dark, abstract shape that seemed to have too many of everything – eyes, legs, teeth, fingers . . . *antennae*.

I dragged my gaze to the three women, and that was when I saw it.

One of them looked like me.

No, it didn't just look like me. It *was* me. I was wearing a crescent moon around my neck, carrying a bow and arrows, and there was a snarling greyhound at my feet.

Diana. It's me as the goddess Diana, fighting this . . .

This.

And sure enough, there was Minerva, carrying a golden spear in one hand and holding an angry-looking owl perched on the other arm. And Vesta – she faced the thing with her bare hands, holding only a blazing torch, which the creature seemed to shrink away from.

I met Vesta's eyes helplessly, actually speechless.

'Spooooky, eh?' Vesta shut the book and steered me to sit down on the couch, before flopping down beside me and putting her boots up on the coffee table. 'It's OK to be freaked out.'

Minerva brought me a steaming teacup, and I took it and held on for dear life.

'Vesta, feet down, please,' said Isobel. 'Well, we should probably begin from the beginning.' She sank down into the second couch, and Minerva sat next to her. 'My name is Isobel Gowdie.'

She paused, as if the name was supposed to mean something to me, and I managed an apologetic smile and a shrug. 'Sorry, not ringing any bells.'

She reached for a very old leather-bound book that was propped up on the arm of the couch and let it fall open to a page that looked like it'd been read many, many times. She held it out to me, and I took it gingerly.

On the left, written in fancy old-fashioned script, were the words *The True Conffefion of Ifobel Gowdie, Witch.*

'Oh you are *kidding me*.' I shook my head as I skim-read the rest of the page.

The red-headed Helsingite had been on point. Isobel Gowdie had been caught by witch-hunters in the 1600s and, unlike most of the others, she'd confessed before they'd had the chance to torture her, spinning an elaborate tale about consorting with devils and speaking to the fairies who lived underground.

A week later, she'd been hung, and then burned as well just to be sure.

There was a woodcut on the opposite page, in case you didn't get the idea. For an old book, it was surprisingly graphic.

I swallowed and leaned back from the book, trying not to imagine what it must feel like to stand among the flames ... but my fingertips seemed glued to the page. I couldn't lift my hands.

Impossible pain shooting through every nerve, blind, deafened by the crackling roar of the flames, I choked on the stink of burning flesh ...

I screamed and the book dropped to the floor in front of me. I shifted back in my seat, half pulling my legs up on to the sofa with me, like a 1950s sitcom housewife who's just seen a rat run across the floor.

'Did you do that?' I snapped.

Isobel scooped the book up gently and laid it beside her. 'No, my dear. You did.'

I glared at her, catching my breath. '*Helpful*. And if I ask if that Isobel was your ancestor, are you going to say something freakish like "no"?'

Isobel folded her hands in her lap and gave me a long, assessing look. 'I won't say it if it disturbs you. But I think you'd rather I gave you a clear answer. I am that same Isobel Gowdie.'

'But you burned,' I whispered. 'I *felt* it.'

Isobel's face went slightly whiter than it already was. 'Then I'm very sorry,' she said quietly. 'I wish I could have spared you that.'

'So, then ... you are a witch. You escaped with magic. Right?' I tried to breathe slowly. I took a sip of my tea. 'And the, um ... all the stuff about ... Satan?'

'Oh, a whole pile of rubbish,' Isobel said quickly. 'I just knew if I kept talking they wouldn't torture me. I told them what they wanted to hear, no more. And, in fact, there are no such things as witches.'

'Says the lady who's claiming to be four hundred years old,' I retorted. 'How did you survive then, how can you still be here?'

Vesta snorted. 'She's got a point, Auntie.'

'There are no such things as witches as you understand them,' Isobel said again, 'but there are other things. I swore an oath, and I cannot die until I have seen it fulfilled. Until I have seen to it that the Witch Pricker is destroyed, and the line of Demon Hunters is safe.'

I felt a muscle in my jaw twitch.

The Witch Pricker returns ...

I stared at Isobel. A four-hundred-year-old non-witch, saved from death by a sacred oath. I *knew* it was crazy, but nothing about it *felt* crazy.

'Minerva, Vesta and I are Demon Hunters,' Isobel said. 'So was your mother, and so are you.'

'I know.' The words were out of my mouth before I could stop them.

Wait, do I? That's news to me ...

Minerva, Vesta and Isobel's eyebrows all shot up.

'I ... I must be. We're the same,' I said, feeling my way through the explanation even as I was saying it out loud. 'The

88

three of us. The painting. And ... and that thing in the dark knew my mother. I've always felt ... *unfinished*. It all makes perfect sense. Well, except ... ' I frowned. 'What the hell *is* a Demon Hunter?'

'We are women who are born with certain special talents,' Isobel said. 'Born to fight evil wherever it appears.'

'You already know what your talent is,' said Minerva.

I stared at her blankly, feeling slow, sifting through the last few days of madness. Then it hit me.

'Oh – the vision-y things? You guys don't get those?'

Minerva and Vesta shook their heads.

Minerva picked up a glass paperweight from a table at her elbow, and held it out to me. There was a little white flower suspended in its depths. I gave her a sceptical look, but took it from her. It was cool and heavy in my hand, perfectly round and smooth. 'Remember when you held the fur, on our stall? And just now, with Isobel's book?'

Of course. The things I'd seen, heard and smelled had been connected to whatever I was holding ...

'I don't think I can make it happen on command,' I said slowly.

'Just relax,' said Vesta, sitting up a little straighter beside me.

'What am I supposed to ... ' I began.

Thin, freezing, foggy mountain air. The cold was like a slap in the face, but the mist rolling over the grass at my feet and the little white flowers that dotted the mountainside all around me were like a roundhouse punch to my sense of reality.

A figure came running out of the mist. Dressed in wool and fur, a crude dagger in her hand, skirt flapping around her knees, she leaped up the rocky hillside towards me. She didn't see me, she simply ran past, the rasping of her breath loud in the silence, and vanished again into the swirling mist ...

The heavy glass paperweight slipped from my fingers and landed on my toe with a *thump*. I jolted back into Isobel's basement sitting room, gasping.

'There, it's OK.' Isobel leaned forwards and took my teacup out of my shaking hand. She set it down carefully and then took both my hands in her wrinkled ones, squeezing gently. 'It must be very disorientating to find your power like this. You should have ... it shouldn't have been like this.'

'I saw a woman, running ...' I shook my head. 'I was *there*. I was on a mountain, *outside*. There were little flowers everywhere, just like the one in the globe, and it was cold.'

Isobel smiled. 'You share the power of your foremothers. For a long time, we have not had an ally with the gift of sight, but now here you are, returned to us, on the day of your sixteenth birthday. A great destiny is at work here.'

'I'm sorry, I have to butt in to say *I told you so*.' Vesta crossed her legs and smiled smugly. 'I said she'd come and neither of you believed me.'

Minerva rolled her eyes. 'Yeah, yeah, we know.'

'You knew I was coming?'

'Call it a wildly optimistic guess,' Minerva said, before Vesta could answer.

'We hoped. But we had no way to know if your family would ever return to Edinburgh,' Isobel said.

'I knew you'd found us as soon as Master Yeun called your name,' Vesta went on, as if the other two hadn't spoken. She leaned forward on her knees, grinning. 'Trinities always have names that match somehow, it's like a ... cosmic side effect. Also we lied about our birthday, it really *is* the same day as yours. *Destiny*,' she said, doing jazz hands for emphasis.

'We tried to tell you the truth, and you thought we were nuts,' Minerva reminded me with a shrug.

I couldn't fault her logic.

'But I have so many more questions. What is the Witch Pricker, is it a demon? Why is there a Witch Pricker if there aren't any witches? Why did it leave a message in my closet? What does it have to do with my mom? Can we just ...' I got up, suddenly short of breath, feeling trapped in the soft cushions of Isobel's sofa. I backed off, my shins smacking against the side of a table, almost sending a taxidermied parrot flying off its perch. I grabbed it to stop its fall and then threw up my hands. 'Can we just call time out, just for a second?'

Isobel stood up slowly – not like an elderly woman struggling with a dodgy hip, but like a queen rising. I took another half step back, leaning against a shelf of cracked leather books. The twins didn't get up: Minerva folded her hands neatly in her lap and Vesta sat straight-backed, her knee jiggling ever so slightly as if she was nervous of what I might do.

'Listen, then, and understand,' Isobel said. 'John Kincaid was a man once – a witch-hunter from my time. They called him the Witch Pricker. He extracted confessions from innocent women, torturing them, pricking their skin with long, wicked needles.'

I shuddered hard. The needles that hung in the darkness of my nightmares ... I could see them in front of my eyes, as clear as if they were here in the room, swaying as Isobel moved towards me ...

I blinked and pinched the skin on my wrist, determined not to zone out in horror.

'Kincaid was an evil man, and demons are drawn to the evil in men's hearts, like leeches to a warm vein,' Isobel said. 'He became possessed, granted powers beyond any mortal man's and set loose on the women of Scotland. I was there, four hundred years ago, when Kincaid captured my friend and sister, your foremother, dearest Elspeth.'

For a moment, Isobel's voice wavered. She reached into a pocket, and pulled out a long silver chain. In the soft blue light from one of the lamps, I could see something hanging from it that glinted and spun. It was a silver hand, open-palmed, fingers slightly splayed.

'We kept her from losing her head to the Maiden, but it was too late,' Isobel said, staring at the silver hand as it turned, reflecting the colours from the lamps, flashing blue and yellow and soft pink. 'She died in Fionna's arms, and our Trinity's powers were broken. Kincaid split his human form, turned to a cloud of moths and fled from us like the coward he truly is. He has been lying low for years, but now you're here, he has finally made his move. And now, finally, we will have our revenge.'

Isobel held out the pendant to me.

'This belonged to Elspeth. It also belonged to your mother. Now, it is yours. Your training must start at once.'

I wanted to help. I also kinda wanted to run for my freaking life.

I took the pendant. Of course I did. But my hand was shaking a little.

I glanced at Vesta and Minerva. They were both smiling, and somehow it steadied me. I slipped the chain around my neck, feeling overwhelmed.

'I know it's a lot to take in. Isobel's been preparing us for this our whole lives,' Minerva said. 'There's a whole bunch of lore and theory and stuff in these books that you can read up on, if you want.'

'*What a nerd*,' Vesta mouthed, shaking her head.

Isobel seemed to be waiting for me to say something.

'So you expect me to fight this demon? With what? A necklace, a brown belt in ju-jitsu and the ability to accidentally transport myself to the past by fondling objects?'

'You've got us,' said Minerva. The twins got to their feet as one. Vesta vaulted the back of the sofa to stand beside me, while Minerva walked around it.

'Demon Hunters come in threes,' Vesta said. She tapped the silver lotus flower at her throat, and I remembered the lightning bolt Minerva had been wearing. 'Now you're here, we have a secret weapon, something even Kincaid is frightened of.'

'When you were with these two in the market, you felt something, didn't you?' said Isobel. 'It would have felt like . . . power, and safety.'

I caught my breath, remembering the slow, loud thumping of my heart and the tension that had fallen away from my shoulders, even when I'd been half convinced I was going to die.

Minerva and Vesta both faced me, and Isobel stood back and folded her arms. 'Now, Diana, make a triangle.'

I raised an eyebrow at her. 'We're in a triangle now. Technically we're always in a triangle,' I added, stubbornness and GCSE Maths kicking in at the same time. 'What kind would you like? Isosceles, right-angle, scalene?' I gave her a slightly desperate smile – to be honest I was pretty impressed with myself for even remembering about scalene. I inched backwards and sideways across the cracked wooden floorboards, looking for the spot where I'd be exactly equidistant from the twins.

When I found it, I stopped smiling and gaped at Isobel, and then at the twins.

There was that feeling again. That warm, stirring, powerful feeling. Now that I knew it was real, it seemed all the stronger. And when I looked up at Minerva and Vesta, they were both wide-eyed, their shoulders back, breathing deeply. It was like a feedback loop: the stronger they looked, the stronger I felt, and the tingling vibration in the air bounced back and forth between us, the air wavering like a heat haze ...

The rash on my wrist suddenly burned with a deep, almost painful itching sensation and I sucked a breath in through my teeth and clamped my hand around it.

I heard two other, identical intakes of breath and looked up to find Minerva and Vesta both cradling their wrists. Vesta looked up at me and gave me a strained, apologetic grin that seemed so impossibly bright I blinked against the glare.

'Oh yeah. I forgot to say. Snap,' she said, holding up her hand so I could see the angry purple mark on her skin.

'That's good.' Isobel took my arm and gently steered me aside, breaking the triangle. The buzzing sensation and the pain in my wrist both stopped. 'That's enough, for the moment. After the bonding, it will be much stronger ...'

She said something else, but I couldn't seem to process her words any more. It was a relief to be rid of the sensory overload, but, at the same time, I instantly missed the feeling of strength and calm. All the energy flooded out of me and I sagged.

'Oop,' said Vesta, and caught my arm, steering me back towards upright. 'I think we've had about all we can handle today.'

'No, I'm fine!' I protested, rather weakly. 'What do we do now? What about Alex?' Saying his name was surprisingly hard. Goosebumps prickled over my arms. How could I be *so wrong*? 'What *is* he?'

'Tomorrow,' said Isobel firmly. 'Vesta's right, you're in no state. The girls will take you home. Diana, listen to me.'

I tried to focus on her face. It was a bit fuzzy.

'If you see the moths, or Kincaid's puppet boy, or *anything* at all out of the ordinary, call us right away. Vesta will put

94

our numbers into your phone.' She hugged me again, softer than before, back in granny mode – or so I thought, until she gripped my shoulders and held me at arm's length. 'Your training begins tomorrow morning. I want you back here at ten. Wear something you can fight in.'

''K,' I said, completely out of words.

I barely remembered climbing the stairs out of Isobel's dim basement or being put into a cab. I know that I was asleep by the time we got to my house because Minerva gently jostled me awake and levered me out of the taxi. I stumbled to the front door and got my key into the lock on the second try.

'See you tomorrow, remember,' Vesta called up the steps after me. I gave a vague wave, and let myself into the hall.

The light inside was so bright I blinked and cringed back.

'Diana!' my dad yelled. 'Where the hell have you been?'

CHAPTER TWELVE

I woke up to the insistent blaring of a hunting horn. I pawed at my phone to get it to stop, and turned over, pulling the pillow over my head.

Then yesterday came back to me like a slap across the face and I sat up gasping.

I'm a what?

Demon Hunter. Hunter of demons.

There was no doubt, no fear that I'd dreamed it all. The silver hand was still resting warm against my skin. And the sensation that had shivered between the three of us, and Isobel's stern, lilting voice ...

I reached over and picked up my book from the bedside table, gingerly sliding out its yellowing paper bookmark.

R would kill me if she knew ... I just want you to know that I love you and I forgive you ... know that we will always be here on Arthur's Seat, keeping watch ...all my love, darling, H

I gaped at the letter, as if seeing it again for the very first time. All these years, I'd wondered what my mom had done to need forgiveness. I still wasn't sure, but it had to be to do with all of this. She'd been a Demon Hunter too, but she'd done something, and then she'd left . . .

I glanced at the photo of Mom that I'd placed on the desk. She looked out at me, a smiling heart-shaped face, black hair pulled into a braid that hung over her shoulder, wearing one of the giant silver Nordic charm necklaces she was so obsessed with.

Did you see visions too?

I wanted my mom then, with a throat-closing intensity I hadn't felt for years. I wanted to talk to her – not just to have her explain, but to share this with someone who already understood.

Last night I saw a woman running over the mountains, and choked on the smoke from Isobel's pyre . . .

And I'd also fallen through a solid wall into a nightmare.

No, not fallen. I was pushed.

The full horror of what Alex had done hit me then. The thought of him shivered down my spine, and I twisted the sheets between my hands.

I'd been *groomed*. There was no other word for it.

My hands trembled as I blotted my wet eyes with the edge of the sheet.

He had picked me out on the train somehow, and he'd reeled me in with cookies and kindness and a pretty face. Because what else could a girl want? Hard abs and a soft voice. I felt bile rising in my throat just thinking about it. He had been *perfect*. And I'd been so certain I could trust him that I'd gone ahead and played the perfect victim.

The worst thing wasn't that he'd turned out to be evil. It was that I'd turned out to be stupid.

Still, there was one upside to this whole situation – I would probably get to punch Alex in his beautiful, lying face.

My phone trumpeted again. I glanced over at it, and a cascade of text messages rolled over the screen before it went dark again.

'Oh God,' I groaned.

Just to top off the best day ever: I'd got into a fight with Dad.

After that first outburst as I came through the door, he'd hugged me tight. Then he had gone deathly calm. He demanded an explanation, but I had none that would make sense. I was too tired to lie, and he was too freaked out to believe a word I said. It wasn't a good combination. Eventually, he got tired of asking questions of someone who was too exhausted to form whole sentences, and sent me to bed, an ominous *we'll talk about this tomorrow* ringing up the stairs behind me.

In the grey light of the morning, I knew he was right to be angry. My phone had been on silent, but that was no excuse, if I'd glanced at it I would've seen I was on the verge of driving him to a nervous breakdown.

I picked up my phone and scrolled grimly through the reams of texts.

Where are you?

We're in the pub, where are you?

Diana are you lost?

I tried to call where are you hon?

Call me back Di

Call back ASAP DIANA

I'm calling the police

I love you.

There were more, but I couldn't face them.

I rolled out of bed, and had just realised that I was still wearing my jeans and socks from last night when my phone blared again.

Oh, right. Someone was texting me now, too. I thumbed into my texts again. The new thread was from a number I didn't remember putting into my phone, but someone had named the contact The Cool Twin.

Wakey wakey Diana!

34 Filigree Street, 10am, wear trackie bottoms and a sports bra.

Text back if you're not dead. V xx

I let out a sigh that was more like a groan and started typing. *Let's at least not repeat yesterday's mistakes . . .*

Not dead. Might be grounded. I'll get back to you.

There was a brief pause, then:

Kincaid's not gonna care. Aunt Isobel says respect your elders. I say climb out a window.

Despite the twisting in my gut, that made me crack a smile.

She was right, even if she was being . . . well, being *Vesta* about it. I'd seen what could happen if I was unprepared. I never, ever wanted to be unprepared again.

I peeled off yesterday's jeans and got dressed in a pair of slouchier dark blue ones and a white tank.

Trusting to reckless optimism, I did put on a sports bra, and I threw some sweat pants and a T-shirt into a backpack before I went downstairs.

Dad was having breakfast at the table in the Starship Kitchen, in the middle of a nest of papers and electronic devices. He seemed to be trying to eat cereal, talk on the phone and type on his laptop all at the same time.

I gave him a tentative smile, trying to look innocent and deeply, genuinely sorry at the same time. He looked up at me and sighed.

'I'm on hold,' he said, gesturing to the phone trapped between his shoulder and his ear. He put it down on the table and tapped the speakerphone button, and the room was suddenly full of tinny Scottish folk music, incongruously cheery.

I thought of the goth-folk, dancing with people in animal masks, leaning against Alex . . . I shuddered.

'Listen, Diana,' Dad said, running his hands through his wild black and grey hair. 'I'm too tired and too busy to fight. Are you going to tell me what you were doing last night?'

I swallowed, a hundred obvious lies flitting through my brain.

'I met some friends, and I just forgot to call you. I'm really sorry,' I said in the end. I don't think Dad believed me, but he wouldn't have believed the truth, either.

A voice interrupted the jaunty music, and Dad's hand twitched for the phone, but it was only a recorded message. *You have reached the National Museum of Scotland. Nobody is available to take your call at the moment. Please stay on the line.*

The music picked back up mid-bar and Dad shook his head. 'I thought you were dead, Diana. I thought you'd been murdered, or . . . anyway, consider yourself on parole. We'll talk punishment later, I don't have time for this today.'

I blinked at him for a second, contrary resentment heating my cheeks as he went back to eating his cereal and typing one-handed.

Wow, Dad. You lose track of me and call the police, but as soon as you're busy you can't even spare a second to ground me. C'mon, 'you're grounded', that would be all you'd have to say. I've been crying you know, look at my face! I'm being evasive. You don't think you should find out what's going on with me? I could be on drugs. I could be dying. You don't know.

You don't want *to know.*

Common sense kicked in before I could accidentally say any of that out loud.

Jeez, Diana. Demons, remember? Take the out.

'I, um ... I should get going, don't want to be late for ju-jitsu. I said I'd stay for extra practice today,' I added quietly, half hoping he wouldn't even hear me.

He gave me a long, cool look, and then the tiniest hint of a smile. 'That's my little warrior,' he said.

I felt slightly dizzy. *My little warrior.* He'd always called me that.

You have no idea.

'You'll keep your phone on, and check in every hour, no excuses,' Dad said, pulling one of the piles of paper towards him and nearly dropping it into his cornflakes. 'And I'll see you later.'

There were stairs in the walls of Isobel's house.

They were hidden behind a tapestry of a stag in the basement. Vesta and Minerva had looked so smug as they led me down, refusing to answer my questions about how exactly we were going to train for anything in Isobel's cluttered sitting room. Now I saw why, and I didn't blame them.

The stairs were built from clean, perfectly solid dark wood, just about wide enough for two of us to walk side by side. There was even plenty of light to climb them by, from bright bulbs set into recesses in the walls.

'These used to be the servants' stairs,' Vesta explained, as we made our way up and around a corner. 'Aunt Isobel had a few extra bits put in a hundred years ago.'

I tried to count the storeys as we climbed, but somehow I couldn't keep them straight in my mind. We seemed to have been going up a long time, the light growing brighter, more like daylight. The walls were white and, when we turned the final corner, I found myself looking up at a door painted a bright, brilliant blue.

Climbing the dark stairs to that door felt like ascending into the clouds. My heart thudded with the anticipation and I found myself thinking about fairy tales and secret doors again. What did Isobel have waiting for us up there?

The twins stood back and let me go through the door first, and I pushed it open and gasped at the room on the other side.

It was a training facility, fully stocked, clean as a spring morning. Real daylight flooded in through a skylight window, and the place *glowed*. The middle of the room was clear, the floorboards polished and sanded. A couple of soft blue mats stood propped up against one wall. There was a standard suspended punching bag, and also a sculpted torso of a man made of rubber. Beside those, a board-breaking table, and – were those slabs of granite?

On the other wall, three archery targets had been set up in a row. Each one looked pocked with holes and slightly singed around the edges. A rack by the door held mock-weapons – swords and spears and daggers made of wood, some with foam padding. A more secure-looking padlocked cabinet held several of the real thing, their sharp edges gleaming.

'Welcome to your destiny, Diana,' said Isobel's voice. I turned to find her standing behind us, framed in the blue doorway. 'Now, let us begin.'

CHAPTER THIRTEEN

'This is amazing,' I said, glee overtaking apprehension. 'You have your own dojo!'

'This place is yours,' said Isobel. She was wearing something like a very upmarket gi, a soft white kimono top embroidered along the sleeves with silver thistles. Her feet were bare. 'Each generation of Demon Hunters must be trained by the last. One day, it will be your turn to train your daughters in the skills they need to defend themselves against the blight of the demon lords.'

I glanced at the twins. They had gone straight to the training mats and were pulling them down, arranging them on the floor.

Where are their *parents?*

And if their mother was one of three, and my mom was the second ... who was the third?

Who were H and R?

Isobel clapped her hands together, breaking up my train of thought. 'Pay attention now, Diana. John Kincaid has found you, and lost you again. He will be coming for all of you.'

Vesta lay the final mat down with a slap and stretched hugely. 'So we need to be ready to kick his demon face in when he does. Him and puppet boy.'

I met her grin with one of my own, my heart still aching just a little at the mention of Alex – or the thing I'd thought was called Alex. But perhaps there was nothing really wrong that punching him in his perfect face wouldn't fix.

For now, I got to train with my new friends, in my own private dojo. This was going to be *fun*.

Minerva pointed out where I should change and I practically skipped over to the corner of the room, slipped behind the screen and tugged on my sweatpants and T-shirt.

By the time I came out, Isobel was standing in the centre of the mats, her white kimono shirt discarded to reveal a simple white vest top and arms with muscles like steel ropes.

'Come,' she commanded, gesturing to the space in front of her. Vesta and Minerva leaned against the wall to my left, their arms folded. 'Don't be alarmed,' said Isobel and, before I could answer, she raised her hands to my face and twisted my head left and right. She tilted my chin, felt around the back of my neck, raised my arms and ran her hand over my spine.

It was like a body search at the airport, only twice as thorough. Isobel's touch was gentle but firm as she prodded, twisted, squeezed and patted me from head to toe. I suppressed a proud smile when she felt along my arms and gave a satisfied 'Hmm!' at the muscle definition, but then she got to my feet and shook her head, sucking her teeth like a mechanic who's found a particularly expensive fault in a brand-new car.

Finally, she straightened up. 'You're in good shape,' she

said. 'Strong. Good muscle mass, good balance. You will be stronger. One shoulder's lower than the other, and your hips are slightly out of whack. Your spine is nice and straight, but you slouch. And you're wearing completely the wrong shoes – you know you have sunken arches, don't you? You're going to have problems with your feet when you're older.'

I blinked at her, not just unaware of my sunken arches, but not completely clear on what sunken arches even were.

Vesta grinned. 'Don't be offended,' she said. 'She's done exactly the same to us. My spine's slightly bent and I've got asthma. Minnie's hypermobile, so if she ever has to wrestle Kincaid we're screwed.'

'Wow.' I thought this over for a second. 'Thank you,' I said eventually, and Isobel gave me a long look – thoughtful, but pleased. 'What are we going to do now?'

'We're going to do some practice with your powers,' she said, and I nearly missed the rest of what she said, because *powers*. 'You have a long road ahead of you – as long as your life. Kincaid, and demons like him, will always try to thwart your attempts to destroy them.'

'And by *thwart you*,' Minerva put in, 'she means *kill you stone dead*.'

Minerva and Vesta walked over to the weapons rack and drew two wooden swords, then leaped into a sparring match, Minerva taking the initiative and getting first strike, but Vesta using her ju-jitsu knowledge to dodge and retaliate swiftly. I could see at once that Minerva didn't have the same type of training as her twin, but she was by no means useless – she handled the sword with a fluid grace that countered and made up for Vesta's wild strength.

'I know how to fight,' I said. 'I've been taking ju-jitsu since I was seven, and—'

I didn't get to finish my sentence. I barely saw Isobel move, there was no tell, no bunching of muscles, before the old lady simply kicked out in a tight circle and hit me in the back of the knee. I yelped and crumpled, too stunned to catch myself so I face-planted straight into the mat. I tried to get up, but stopped, gaping at Isobel as she threw herself into a perfect mid-air forward roll, flipping over me and landing on the mat behind me. I tried to twist around, but one of her arms clamped around my throat and one of her knees dug into the small of my back.

'What are you going to do now?' she said.

I wanted to choke or yelp, to curl around the pain, but any move I could make would either close my own windpipe or bruise my own spine. Isobel wouldn't have to move a muscle. My arms were free, but close to useless. I could try to catch her hair or elbow her in the face …

I held very still for a few seconds, and then said, as politely as I could manage, 'Could I tap out, please?'

Behind me, Isobel chuckled. The pressure eased, and then she let me go and I rolled over on to my face and gasped into the surface of the mat.

Minerva and Vesta paused in their swordfight to burst into simultaneous, spontaneous applause.

'Girls, one more point and then join us here.' She rose lightly to her feet and held out a hand to help me up. I took it gratefully. 'I need you to understand how much further you have to go. If you're not prepared to face the demon, it will kill you. And it will eat your souls,' she added solemnly. 'And probably your liver and eyeballs, as well.'

She had to be kidding. I tried for a smile, and she gave a small shake of her head.

Holy crap. She's not kidding.

I rubbed my throat where she'd had me pinned. Sparring with new friends in a beautiful sunlit room in the middle of the day ... it would be easy to believe that this was all there was to it, that the thing in the black room had just been some horrible dream, but I wasn't enough of a fool to pretend that was the truth.

'So, this witch-hunter, Kincaid. He's a man, but there's a demon inside him?'

'That's right,' Isobel said. 'Demons take on a human vessel – part disguise, part shield for their true form.'

'Where do they come from? Is it ... you know ...?'

'Nobody knows what's on the other side of the veil,' Isobel said. 'Perhaps it is Hell, perhaps it's just some other world like ours. But there are places where the veil is thin and, when it tears, one of Them can come through to our world.'

'But what are we actually facing here? Shouldn't we be learning exorcisms and stocking up on holy water or something rather than training to fight?'

'Believe me,' Isobel said, 'if the trappings of faith were any help to us, this would be much easier. No – our strength comes from *somewhere*, but you must rely only on yourselves. Once you've been through the bonding ceremony, you should be able to force the demon out of the shell of Kincaid's body.'

'Bonding ceremony?' I asked, trying to process all of this, get it locked down inside. *Break the shell, force the demon out ... don't die.*

'You'll go there tonight, after we're done here,' Isobel said. 'The three of you need to become a Trinity, a sisterhood, bonded by more than blood. It takes a little more than wearing matching necklaces. Don't worry,' she added, 'it doesn't hurt.'

I was unconvinced.

'And if we do get the demon out of Kincaid, then what?' I asked, trying not to think about the many-legged, many-faced dark creature from the painting of the three goddesses.

'Then we kill it,' said Minerva, with a quiet confidence that gave me chills. 'It'll have to take form outside Kincaid, and that means it'll die like any other living thing.'

'You say that,' I muttered. 'Have you ever killed a demon? Have you killed ... anything? I haven't! I don't know if I ...'

'Kincaid has,' Isobel said, her voice low. 'His demon has. Hundreds of innocent lives, Diana. Maybe thousands. You *will* learn to kill. You are the only ones who can stop him.'

'Stop him from doing what?' I demanded. 'It's not like he can just go around burning people nowadays.'

'You don't think so?' Isobel asked. She quirked an eyebrow at me. 'Truly, you think there are no men in this enlightened century who would welcome the opportunity to abuse and kill?'

That shut me up.

'Kincaid is vain, but the demon doesn't care for grand gestures,' Isobel went on. Outside the attic skylight the sun slipped behind a cloud, and I shivered. 'It craves the blood and terror of human beings. Where the demon walks, evil breeds. Perhaps instead of beheading women in the public square he would have his lackeys blow them up, or shoot them with guns. But have no doubt, he would find a willing and receptive audience for his hate, he would turn their weakness into a lust for blood, and you would see death on a scale you cannot imagine.'

She watched me expectantly, but I couldn't speak – I could barely breathe. Eventually, Vesta took pity on me.

'Come on, tell her,' she said, and swung her wooden sword up to rest across her shoulders. 'Tell her how come we're not all living in that dystopia already.'

'The demon is afraid of *you*,' said Isobel. 'It knows your strength, Diana, even if you do not, and it is so afraid that

108

it would rather send a puppet boy to lure you in than come out and face you itself. Why don't you two show Diana what you've been working on?' she added, taking a firm hold of my elbow and leading me off the mat, away from the twins.

Minerva nodded and shook out her hands and feet, then turned to face the wall with the straw-stuffed archery targets ranged along it. She began to mutter under her breath, lilting words in a language I didn't recognise, and fixed her eyes on the yellow circle at the centre of the target.

What's she going to do? She hasn't got a bow or a throwing knife or any—

Minerva threw out her hand towards the targets and I flinched back with a yelp as white fire arced from her fingertips. It flickered for a second and then vanished, leaving a glowing after-image on the back of my eyes. I blinked at the target. Minerva had hit it, that was for sure. It was on fire. Minerva hurried over with a mini fire extinguisher and blasted at the target until there was just a thick black scorch mark in the blue circle near the left edge.

What do you even say to something like that?

'Your aim still needs a lot of work,' said Isobel. I guessed that was one way to put it.

'What language was that?' I managed.

'Old Gaelic,' Minerva said, breathing heavily. 'It's not really about the words, but I find them useful to channel my thoughts into the right shapes.'

'OK,' I said, as if I understood anything she'd just said.

Vesta stepped towards the breaking boards, and picked up one of the granite slabs. But she didn't lay it down on the table – she took a deep breath, centred herself, and then broke the slab in two over her knee.

'Woah!' I cried, exhaling my wonder in a single explosive breath.

Vesta grinned and took a bow. 'Thank you, thank you.'

'Did I even actually beat you in class?' I asked, stunned, 'Or did you just let me win?'

'No, you really did,' Vesta admitted. 'Super-strength doesn't come with super-fast reflexes, sadly. Once you had me in an arm-bar, I basically had the option of tapping out or breaking your legs. I don't think that would've gone down well with Master Yeun.'

'So, let me get this straight – Minerva can shoot lightning from her fingers and Vesta is super-strong, and I'm ...?'

'You're the Seer,' said Isobel.

'And that's helpful how?'

'Once you can control your power, it will be hugely helpful,' Isobel tried to reassure me, but I was shaking my head, suddenly feeling like I had drawn not just the short straw but the only straw in a big pile of magic swords. 'Many powerful Hunters have had this power before you, including Elspeth.'

I remembered that they were friends just in time to stop myself pointing out that it didn't do Elspeth much good.

'Try it,' Isobel encouraged, gesturing widely around the room at the training equipment. 'You should be able to See with any object you desire. Pick one.'

I swallowed, walked over to the rack of wooden swords and gingerly reached out to draw one from its place, feeling like King Arthur pulling the sword from the stone.

Nothing happened as my palm made contact. I held the sword in my hand, stared at it and breathed deeply.

Still nothing happened.

I concentrated until I could feel the muscles in my jaw jumping with the tension, trying to remember how I had felt right before I'd Seen. I'd been curious, anxious, excited ...

There was nothing those moments had in common except that I wasn't trying to 'See'.

So I tried not to try, but, of course, that didn't work either.

Minerva, Vesta and Isobel were all standing quietly by while I stared down at the wooden sword, very politely not laughing as I pulled some pretty stupid faces. They said and did nothing to distract me, which became more and more distracting as more and more absolutely nothing happened.

I stood there trying to mentally fondle the sword for as long as I could bear to, then flipped it back into the rack with a loud *thunk*.

'So, what am I doing wrong?' I demanded, turning to Isobel. 'Because I'm getting nothing. Not a whiff. All I had to do was take the book from you and then I was *on fire*. What's my mistake?'

I knew what she was going to say before she said it. It was written on her face. 'I don't know.'

'Of course you don't.' I shook my head.

'You just have to practice,' Minerva said. 'We've been doing hours of training every day since our powers came through.'

'And that's just the powers,' Vesta added. 'Isobel's had us doing an hour a day on the other stuff since we were four.'

'And we knew that we'd get powers, too,' Minerva went on. 'And it still wasn't easy. For weeks I was just giving off this constant static and making all our hair stand on end. You just need a little time to catch up. If we're careful, we'll have time to help you get it before we have to face Kincaid, right?'

Isobel nodded. 'I have a training programme drawn up. I'd like you to come and live here with us until it's finished – but I don't suppose you'll want to leave your father,' she added.

Well . . . maybe I wouldn't mind as much as you think. It wouldn't be like moving out for ever. Just long enough for me to get a handle on who I was now. Who I was going to be. It would be like going off to college, but only for a month, or however long Isobel had in mind for a crash course in demon hunting.

111

And instead of a final exam, I had to kill a demon and save the world.

It was a nice thought, but how would I explain it to Dad? Also we were coming on for 11.30, I should text him to check in ...

'I can't,' I said, rather reluctantly. 'And I don't think he'd be up for moving in here, somehow.'

'No, that certainly isn't an option,' said Isobel. 'So you will simply have to come here for your training. We'll workshop your route and escape options if Kincaid strikes at you on your way. And whatever you do, do not go anywhere near the museum or the Maiden. Kincaid will have left that poor woman's head there for a reason.'

I cringed, feeling stupid that I hadn't put that together yet ... and then I groaned.

'There might be a problem. My dad's investigating that severed head.'

'Investigating?' Isobel frowned. 'Is he with the police?'

'He's a writer. I mean, people call him a ghost-hunter, but I don't think he has any idea that all this is going on,' I added, gesturing widely to take in Isobel, the twins, the demons, everything.

'You must stop him,' Isobel said. 'That little piece of demonic theatre is meant for us. Kincaid will be hiding nearby, but we mustn't rush into making our move.'

'What can I do?' I said. 'I can't exactly tell him to stop looking into it because it's a real demon. That'll just make him run at it with everything he has – if he even believes me,' I added.

'Do whatever you have to,' Isobel said sternly. 'When you return home after the ceremony, you *must* stop him.'

I texted Dad –

Still alive, Dxxx

– and then Isobel started on the evasive drills.

The drill was like some kind of catch-all nightmare scenario escape practice. Run on the spot, jump, down to the floor, roll, up, dodge left, left again, right, down, then run on the spot some more, and then punch out or avoid dodgeballs, which she would throw randomly at our faces, and then drop and roll and dodge and run. Now again, but in double-time.

The afternoon wore on, and I started to see what Isobel's intensive training was going to have in store for me – drills, then weapons practice. Then a break, which I spent lying on the floor making distressed whale noises. Then meditation and t'ai chi. Then dinner, and then, blessed be, a short nap in a spare bed with a taxidermy crow looming over me.

I left it as late as I could to call Dad and say not to wait up – this wasn't going to be the kind of argument you could have by text – but when I finally did it, he didn't pick up.

Oh, OK. I'm going to take that as a yes . . .

'Hey, Dad,' I said after the beep, 'some girls from the club invited me back to theirs for pizza and they invited me to stay the night. That's OK, right? I mean, since I'm on parole. You can totally call if it's not OK, but I might be out of signal. Love you! Bye.'

The lying was a bit disturbingly easy.

He didn't call back, so I didn't feel too guilty about setting my alarm for 2.30 a.m. and collapsing back into bed. When it went off I levered myself up, pulled on my boots and my red jacket, and met Vesta and Minerva in the hall.

'Our ride's here,' said Minerva. 'You ready?'

'If it involves dodgeballs I'm all set,' I said. 'Although you still haven't told me where we're going.'

Vesta clamped a hand on my shoulder and squeezed. 'We're going to accept our destiny.'

CHAPTER FOURTEEN

The street lights outside Isobel's house were weak and the moon was hidden behind thick cloud, so it was nearly pitch dark when we stepped outside. I clutched my jacket around myself, shivering. Summer Solstice or not, 3 a.m. was a bad time to be wandering around the streets of Edinburgh.

I looked out on to the street, and realised there was somebody outside the house, leaning on a car, watching us. I jumped, my heart rate through the roof, imagining that Alex had found us and we would have to fight him right here, now, in the middle of a suburban Edinburgh street. But then my eyes adjusted to the dim light, and recognised that the silhouette was totally different. This boy was also about our age, but he was shorter and thinner, with a head of curly hair and a fringe that fell over one side of his face.

'About time too,' he said, pushing his hand through the fringe as we came down the steps. It bounced right back. He was wearing a sort of shabby *Brideshead Revisited* get-up, with cream trousers and a shirt with the sleeves rolled up, a knitted tank top and glasses – I couldn't tell if they were lensless hipster posing glasses or real ones.

'This is Sebastian,' said Vesta.

Of course it is, I thought.

Vesta pointed affectionately in his face. 'Be careful around this one, he's a bad influence.'

Sebastian's cheeks flushed darkly. 'Hi, Vesta,' he said. His eyes followed her as she threw open the car door and slid into the back seat.

'Hi. I'm Diana,' I said, holding out my hand. He turned back to me, and his expression clouded over. He paused, just long enough for it to feel awkward, before he shook my hand.

'I know who you are,' he said, without smiling. He seemed to be looking me up and down, a little judgementally for someone who – I could see now – did not have any lenses in his glasses. I smiled aggressively at him.

'Well great, that makes one of us,' I said. 'Who exactly are you? What did she mean, a bad influence?'

Sebastian glanced at Vesta getting comfy on the back seat and got that flustered look again, and I couldn't help feeling a little more kindly towards him. I knew an intense crush when I saw one.

'She's not wrong. Seb's a terror to society. You'll see,' said Minerva, getting in after Vesta with a nod in Sebastian's direction.

'I really hope it's not because of your driving,' I said, looking at the car. It was a Mini – but not one of the sleek, sporty modern ones. It was blocky and vintage – 1970s, maybe – the paint was a shabby red, and the body looked like it was made of tinfoil. I hesitated. Really, we were going to

115

drive around Edinburgh in this? Surely it would collapse into a pile of sheet metal at the first sign of a strong wind.

Sebastian probably read the look on my face, because he looked like I'd insulted his mother as he walked around to the driver's side. He patted the roof of the car. It gave a slightly discouraging *clang*.

'Don't worry yourself,' he said. 'Ruby's been ferrying Hunters around since 1971.'

'Yeah ... that's pretty much what I'm worrying about,' I said, which made Sebastian glare daggers at me again. I opened the tinfoil door and eased myself down into the shabby leather passenger seat anyway. The inside of the car smelled like rust, oil and bacon. The interior was so basic I wondered for a minute if a car could even operate with so few buttons – there were old-fashioned dials measuring speed and petrol levels, a steering wheel, foot pedals and a gear stick, and that was basically it, apart from a sleek, out-of-place looking portable phone speaker dock sitting in the ample space under the dashboard.

Sebastian wrenched the gear stick around and Ruby's engine came alive with a surprisingly smooth chugging sound, and we eased away from the kerb. I turned to look back up at the house, and thought I caught a flash of white hair at an upstairs window, but then it was gone.

'So ... how come Isobel didn't come with us?' I asked, twisting in my seat to look at the twins. 'Surely she's the only one here who knows how this ... um ... ' I faltered, glancing at Sebastian, suddenly uncertain how much he knew, or ought to know. He'd mentioned Hunters, so he had to be safe, right?

'The bonding ceremony,' Minerva said, with a small nod, and I relaxed slightly. 'Aunt Isobel ... doesn't get out much. She actually doesn't leave the house. Ever.'

'*Ever?*'

'Not unless it's really, really serious,' Minerva said. 'She's got a few things in there she says she can't risk leaving, no matter what.'

I thought of the secret stairway, and wondered if that wasn't the only secret passageway Isobel had access to.

'She does wish she could be here for our bonding,' Vesta said. 'But she's told us what to do, we just have to get up to the summit, and stand in our positions, like we did in the basement yesterday. It should just happen.'

'What, no magic words or anything?'

'Nope.' Vesta shrugged. 'Auntie says it's a force of nature thing.'

'Well, OK.' I settled back into my seat. 'We're not going to break into the Castle or anything, are we?' I added, trying to think of the highest outdoor point in Edinburgh, and not liking the answer my brain had supplied.

Minerva chuckled. 'Did you not see Arthur's Seat on the way here?' she asked. 'You'll have passed it if you came up on the train.'

I tried to remember. 'I don't think so. I was reading,' I added, although the words felt hollow. It was true, I'd been pretty focused on bringing down a fictional dystopian state. But 'I was reading' wasn't the whole story. I shuddered.

I was trying not to stare at Alex. I was drinking the coffee he bought me and eating his biscuits and trying to look normal so that he wouldn't think I was weird for dreaming about the puppet master who was pulling his strings all along.

'Tiny little lumpy mountain? Right as you come into town? No?' Sebastian prompted. I frowned. We were going up a *mountain*? 'Oh yeah, you clearly weren't paying attention, you would definitely remember.'

The car swerved around a corner and I put a hand out to

steady myself on Ruby's plastic and chrome dashboard. As my palm made contact, I half tried to open my mind, to let in whatever visions or sensations wanted to come to me from the demon-hunting days of the early 1970s. But I didn't feel a thing.

'So, if you don't mind me asking,' I turned to Sebastian, 'how come you're here? I mean, picking us up in the middle of the night and driving us off to do a magic ritual? What's your connection to all of this?'

There was an awkward pause. Sebastian glared at the road in his headlights and didn't reply for a second.

What was this guy's problem?

'I'm family. My mum was a Demon Hunter,' he said. His voice was steady, but cold. I noted the past tense, and started to say I was sorry, but he went on. 'So you're Kara's daughter.'

'Don't, Seb,' said Minerva from the back seat, so quietly I almost didn't hear her over the thrum of Ruby's engine.

'My mum was Rota McKay,' Sebastian said. 'Did Kara ever mention her?'

'I don't think so. My mom died when I was six,' I said.

I regretted it immediately, even before Sebastian said, 'Mine died when I was ten. The twins were nine when their mum passed away.'

I glanced back at the twins. Vesta was staring out the window at the streets crawling by, while Minerva was watching us – she gave a sad half-smile, and changed the subject.

'Only three female Demon Hunters can form a Trinity like we're going to do, and only a Trinity can truly defeat demons. But Isobel's always trained up Hunter kids in Edinburgh, boys and girls, to do what we can just in case there's mischief we can handle.'

'It's just the three of us now,' Sebastian pointed out. 'I'm an only child. If you hadn't happened to come back when you did, these two would have been stuffed.'

I shifted awkwardly in my seat, biting back a *you're welcome*, wondering what had made this boy so bitter. Did he just wish he could be one of us, was that it?

'I keep telling you, it's destiny,' said Vesta.

'*Destiny*'s not—' Sebastian snapped, then shook his head. 'Anyway you can think of Demon Hunter boys as . . . support staff.'

'So you don't have powers?' I asked.

'I wouldn't say that,' Vesta said knowingly.

Sebastian went red again.

The buildings were changing around us now, as we left the dark suburbs and started to skirt the city centre. We stuck to the main roads, and there weren't many other cars around, but it was much brighter here. The Solstice Festival was over a full day ago, but there were still a few people who clearly weren't ready to give it up. We stopped at a red light and a group of people in masks crossed the road in front of us, laughing and leaning on each other, wall-eyed rabbits and cats, and even a horse.

Then suddenly, there was a bang on the window by my head, and I jumped out of my skin and turned to see a pair of jaws pressed up to the window, beady human eyes blinking behind the cut-out eyeholes of a red fox.

Isobel's evasive drills kicked in and I leaned away from the window, barging against Sebastian as I tried to get in position to kick the intruder in the balls if he opened the car door.

The fox laughed and ran over to join his friends. I stared at him, aghast and angry and relieved that he was just some troll in a rubber mask. Vesta wound down the window and gave him the finger and a piece of her mind, in language that I was pretty sure would make Isobel's head explode.

'Can we avoid Grassmarket?' I blurted suddenly, and then felt stupid – did I think Alex would still be there, looking for me, a whole day after I'd ditched him?

'We're not going that way. We're going up along Princes Street and down again, it's quicker.'

I breathed easier anyway as we turned off that road and left the animals behind. I was so not ready to face Alex yet. I sat a little lower in my chair, trying not to let myself worry about what he'd done when he'd found out I had gone.

We threaded through the streets and past darkened shops, tall monuments that glinted in the street lights, and enormous looming buildings.

'On your right,' Sebastian said, in a voice like one of the tour guides you get on open-top buses, the kind who are relentlessly cheery even when it's pouring with rain, 'you will see the modern Scottish Parliament building.'

I peered out of the window at a blocky white structure in the sweeping concrete and glass school of architecture.

'And on your left in just a second,' said Vesta, picking up the imaginary mic, 'you will catch a glimpse of the ancient and beautiful Palace of Holyroodhouse.'

A pair of pretty, curling metal gates flashed by: I could make out a slightly castle-ish tinge to the buildings beyond.

'And, finally, if you look straight ahead,' Sebastian said, 'you will see Holyrood Park, home of Arthur's Seat, which may once have been the location of King Arthur's castle Camelot, but probably wasn't.'

For a minute I couldn't see anything ahead, and then I realised that it was because there was nothing there. No buildings, no city lights, just dark cliffs that rose abruptly out of the ground. It was midsummer, and dawn was already on its way, so the sky seemed a slightly lighter shade of black than the shadowy earth.

Sebastian swung Ruby around a mini roundabout and, when we'd righted ourselves again, I stared out at the landscape on my left in wonder, making out a few trees and scrubby bushes, but mostly just grass and rock. If there was a summit, I couldn't see it from here.

The road circled around the edge of the park a little way, and then we slowed and pulled off into a dark parking lot beside a small lake.

We piled out of the car. Sebastian went around to the back to take something out of the trunk, and the twins and I stood in silence for a moment, staring up the hill.

'The summit's pretty much directly ahead,' Minerva said, and her voice was loud in my ear now that the only other sound was the quiet hum of the city as it slept fitfully all around us.

I couldn't quite believe that we were just going to head off up this hill, before dawn, with no idea what kind of 'force of nature' we were supposed to be unleashing at the top. We were feeling our way blind, in more ways than one.

It felt scary ... and amazing. I suddenly flashed back to walks through the forests of northern California, running ahead of Mom and Dad, plastic bow and quiver of arrows over my shoulder, playing at hunting for stags and bears. My parents were my servants, obviously, who would carry the carcass back home when I finally caught something. I remembered feeling like my heart was full, like I was right where I was always meant to be – at least until I slipped in a puddle or walked into a spiderweb and started longing to feel pavement under my feet again.

Whenever we moved house, Dad said it was going to be an adventure, but it always turned out to be disappointingly real – new buses, schools and currencies, and a million boring forms to fill in.

But you were right, Dad, I thought, looking up at the craggy hillside. *This time, you were actually right. I'm having an adventure.*

'Are you ready?' Sebastian had thrown a long, heavy-looking canvas bag over his shoulder. It was nearly as long as he was tall, and it hung awkwardly as he walked.

'To walk up a hill?' I teased. 'Dude, I'm from San Francisco. I was born ready.'

Sebastian looked at the twins. 'Is she?'

'She's in, Sebastian, leave it alone,' Minerva said.

Sebastian shrugged and set off, the bag hanging heavy on his shoulder.

We started across the road and stepped out into this little piece of wilderness. The slope wasn't too steep at first and it was an easy stroll, keeping to the path by the light of the slowly brightening sky. The air seemed fresher as soon as we'd left the road, which was probably an illusion, and smelled of wet greenery and dog mess, which probably wasn't.

Sebastian strode ahead, hefting the bag back up on to his shoulder every few steps. After about two hundred yards, Vesta ran a few steps to catch up with him. They were far enough ahead that I couldn't hear their conversation, but Vesta had plunged her hands into the pockets of her trench coat and tossed back her hair, and, a minute or two later, they paused and Sebastian handed over the bag. Vesta took it, swung it over her shoulders and strode easily onwards as if it was no heavier than my plastic bow and arrows.

'What's up with him, anyway?' I said to Minerva, who was walking quietly at my side and looking up at the sky. 'And how come he only has to look at Vesta and he suddenly turns all cute?'

'It's sweet, isn't it?' she said. 'I'm sorry he's being a bit

122

stand-offish, he's really not at all like a wanker when you get to know him. He just ... He's very protective of us.'

'Especially Vesta, I bet.'

'Oh yeah. It's so obvious, I don't know how she's managed to miss it.'

'What, really?'

'Yep. She's totally oblivious.'

I looked up again at Sebastian, who was bending his head attentively towards something Vesta was saying. '*How?*'

'She can be really dense,' Minerva said, with an affectionate smile.

'Why doesn't he just say something? Does she have a boyfriend?'

'No, he's just painfully shy about it. I think he thinks if she says no to dating him their friendship will be broken for ever and he'll die of a broken heart.'

'Well that's dumb.'

Minerva grinned at me. 'Maybe you can talk some sense into him, then. I've never had any luck. Still,' she added contemplatively, 'it could have been worse. He could have fallen for the twin who wasn't into boys, you know, as a genre.'

'Ha! Still, at least you would've given him a nice clean "no". "Nothing personal, just not into your entire gender."'

Minerva laughed. 'I guess that's true. Don't get me wrong,' she added, 'I also wouldn't date Seb if he was a girl. I'm just not that into the lovesick puppy look.'

'And Vesta?' I asked, lowering my voice as Vesta and Sebastian hit a steeper part of the path and slowed down in front of us. 'Straight, tick, unattached, tick – how does she feel about puppies?'

'Oh, when she finally figures it out she's going to love it. Isobel, perhaps not so much.'

'What? Why?'

'Well, it's not really *done*, to mix Hunter lines like that. Reduces the chance of there being enough girl babies born for the next generation's Trinity ... not that dating each other exactly means you have to end up getting married and having babies, but that's how Isobel thinks. Always looking out for the Line.'

I nodded, the implications of all this hitting me slowly as I stepped carefully over a heap of loose stones. Isobel wanted to safeguard the next generation. She'd want us all to have children, preferably girls, and that included me. Was I really ready to give some four-hundred-year-old stranger that kind of control over my life? My steps slowed a little and I stared up at the dark line of the summit, suddenly feeling cold.

'Of course, Isobel doesn't have much of a leg to stand on after the drama with Mum and Dad,' Minerva went on. 'He was a Hunter boy, and she disapproved, but they got married, and then bam: twins. Problem solved. Destiny's like that.'

'So, if you don't mind me asking ...' I stuck my hands in my pockets and fixed my eyes on the pebbly earth beneath my feet. 'How is she about you being gay?'

'She had a bit of a flaïl about it at first,' Minerva said, cheerfully. 'Then I pointed out that I probably do want kids and IVF is a thing, and she calmed right down.' In the dark, I could just make out her fond smile – and the steely quirk of her eyebrows. It steadied me.

Perhaps my future is partly written. Perhaps we do have a duty. But our choices are still our own ...

We lapsed into thoughtful silence as the terrain got slightly steeper, and I paused to look back the way we'd come. We'd climbed surprisingly high already, and I could see over the roofs of the houses, past the street lights to the bay and the dark sea.

When I turned back, the sky was light enough that the hill in front of me stood out as a sharp, dark shadow. I blinked up at the summit, Arthur's Seat itself, slightly stunned. It was so odd-looking – a big square-ish rock formation, standing up proud from the land around it, almost like a smaller version of the red rock mesas in the California desert.

We climbed onwards, up and over ridges in the hillside. The land became more rocky and the grass grew thinner. It wasn't long before we were on the final ascent up a steep path to the top of the Seat. Oddly, it seemed to have grown darker in the last few minutes, and I looked up and saw that the lightening sky was suddenly full of thick, dark clouds.

'Are those storm clouds?' I asked and, as Minerva looked up to see, my question was answered with a distant rumble and a fat drop of rain landing right on my cheek.

'Perfect,' Minerva whispered and, to my slight dismay, she wasn't being sarcastic.

The top of Arthur's Seat was rocky and uneven. We climbed over the red ledges and slippery stones until we came to the summit marker – a white concrete block liberally covered in graffiti. Vesta laid down the canvas bag with a *clank*.

I hurried to the far edge of the plateau to look out over the sleeping city before it was shrouded by the curtain of rain. The view was stunning – a blanket of twinkling orange lights, threaded with roads and studded with tall spires and, right in the centre, the Castle perched on its hilltop over the ravine.

I took a second just to drink it all in, and then turned to find the others looking out on it too, all smiling, despite the rain that was starting to patter down regularly around us.

'What's it like,' I wondered aloud, '*living* in a place like this? I mean, what's it like to look at a view like this and say, yep, that's my home?'

125

'It's amazing,' Vesta said, with genuine feeling. 'You're going to love it.'

That's right. I live here now. Not just for a year, or two, until Dad decides to chase after some other city's ghosts. My life is here.

It should have been a frightening feeling – it was so *fast*, less than a week after I'd arrived and I was already planning out the rest of my life, short as it might be. But it wasn't frightening at all. I was *ready*.

'Are you?' said Sebastian, breaking into my train of thought.

I blinked and looked over at him. The rain was getting heavier now, and he blinked as a drip fell from his fringe and into his eyes.

'What?'

'Are you going to love it here? Are you going to stay if you don't?'

'Sebastian, I swear, I will throw you off this cliff,' Vesta sighed. 'She's here, isn't she? She's literally just moved here and she's up on this mountain with us in the rain, let's just do it!'

Sebastian rounded on her. 'I don't think she has any idea what she's signing up for! I think you and Isobel are rushing her through this because you don't want to give her time to change her mind. What if you're bonded and then she just up and *leaves*?'

'She's not her mum!' Minerva snapped.

'Hey!' I yelled.

They all turned to look at me.

I crossed my arms, trying not to shiver. 'Enough. You talk about me like I'm not here again, I'm going back down right now and I'm not bonding with anybody.'

Sebastian threw his hand up, as if to say, *See?*

Vesta hesitated, tucking her trench coat around herself and glancing at Minerva. For the first time since we'd met, she didn't seem to know what to say. 'We ... we're not going to go over this now, are we?' she muttered. 'I don't think Isobel wanted ...'

'Vesta, look at me. What did my mom do?' I said.

'It's complicated,' said Vesta.

'She betrayed us,' said Sebastian.

CHAPTER FIFTEEN

'My mum and Hilde are both dead because of her.' Sebastian spoke slowly, clearly, so there could be no mistake. I felt as if he'd dropped the words on me from a great height.

Mom?

She had done something, I always knew that, but ... no, I refused to believe it.

My mom, who was a San Francisco hippy at heart if not by birth. She was kind. She loved to point out bugs and people who were happy and flowers that grew in cracks in the pavement: telling signs of life that the rest of us would miss. She walked into haunted houses at Dad's side, and I was never afraid for her.

Then a large, heavy raindrop splashed on my nose and I shook my head, spraying water from my tightening curls like a dog coming out of the ocean.

'Hilde – is that your mom?' I asked, turning to Minerva. She nodded. 'Rota and Hilde.' I half smiled, despite the freezing rain soaking into my jeans and Sebastian's frown. 'A long time ago, my mom got a letter from someone who just signed themselves "H". It said H forgave my mom, but "R" would be angry if she knew H was writing.'

'Your mum ... ran away,' said Minerva softly. 'She never went through with the bonding ritual. Hilde and Rota and Kara were supposed to be a Trinity. They were the only girls in that generation, born on the same day, named for a trio of Valkyries ... all the signs were there. But Kara left, right before they turned sixteen.'

'She abandoned her destiny,' Sebastian said. 'She abandoned her friends when they needed her. Our parents were left without their full powers, without any way of stopping the demon. They defended this world to their very last breaths, while Kara ran off to live happily ever after in sunny California.'

'She wanted to *live*,' Minerva said. She folded her arms and shivered. 'This is serious, Sebastian – you can't know what it's like to be one of us. Kara was right to be afraid.'

'Our parents got over it,' Sebastian muttered, kicking a red rock and sending up a splash of rainwater. 'Kara was the only one who was a coward.'

I bristled at that. 'I bet it took guts to tell Isobel no! Mom chose to deny her entire destiny. I've only had one about twelve hours and I *feel* how hard that must have been!' I thought of the power that flowed between the twins and me, thought of never ever feeling that again, and genuinely shuddered.

'Sebastian, you have to face it,' Vesta said, scraping her wet hair back out of her face and planting her hands on her hips, 'it wasn't Kara's fault Mum and Rota were killed, and it's no way Diana's fault. You want to talk about destiny – if Kara hadn't left, she wouldn't have met Di's dad, she wouldn't have been born, and we wouldn't be here right now. You don't know what's meant to be!'

Sebastian shrank under the heat of Vesta's glare, and his expression twisted, sadness elbowing his anger aside. 'She left her friends when they needed her most,' he said again, and gave me a look that was more pleading than accusing. 'How can I know you won't do the same?'

I took a deep breath, staring down at the dark red earth where the rain was dancing between the stones. 'You can't know,' I said. I looked up at Sebastian, and I thought about what the Kara I knew would say right now, and I gave him a kind and genuine smile. 'You don't know anything about me. But you're going to have loads of time to find out. Because we're doing this.'

I brushed the damp hair out of my eyes. 'What's in the bag, Vesta?'

'Ask Seb,' she said.

Sebastian hesitated, and then knelt down and opened the bag, to reveal ...

Weapons. I peered down, spotting leather sheaths and polished black handles, and Sebastian held up a hand as if to block my view.

'No, don't look! You'll ruin the surprise.'

'Is it going to be fun surprise?' I asked. 'Or more of a cold, stabby surprise?'

'Bit of both,' he said, rain spattering on his glasses as he fished carefully in the bag. 'It's a present, from Isobel – and me, too,' he added, reluctantly. 'For your sixteenth birthday, and on this, the occasion of your eternal bonding to these two nutbags.'

'We've already had ours,' Vesta said. Sebastian pulled out a strange, round object and handed it to Vesta. She took it and tugged off the tight leather sheath to reveal a perfect, near-circular silver sickle.

Minerva bent down to take her own weapon. It was stashed

in a drawstring bag, and when she took it out it didn't look like anything much – just a pile of sleek black pieces of metal. But then she hit a hidden switch, and it unfolded in a scary-smooth motion with a sharp twang. It was a modern-looking collapsible crossbow.

'All right, shut your eyes, Diana,' Sebastian said. 'And hold out your hands.'

I paused, meeting his gaze for a few more wet seconds.

I trust you. You haven't given me all that much reason to, but I'm going to anyway. Return the favour, OK?

I squeezed my eyes shut and held my hand out, intensely aware that if I was as wrong about these people as I had been about Alex, they could now stab me, shoot me and throw me off a mountain.

Something heavy was lowered down on to my palms. I paused for a moment before I opened my eyes, feeling its weight, its pleasantly smooth roundness. I felt almost meditative, with the rain pattering down on my face.

I opened my eyes, and gasped at the beauty of the thing in front of me. It was a naginata – I'd seen them used in mixed martial arts competitions, and in pictures of ancient Japanese warriors.

The naginata was a sword-staff with a long, black lacquered handle nearly as tall as I was and a blade that reached up above my head and bent back at the end to form a cutting edge and, on the backswing, a vicious stabbing point. Gold threads wound around the black handle to form a grip.

'It's beautiful,' I breathed. I gave it an experimental swing, careful not to catch Sebastian or the twins in its wide arc. It was perfectly balanced, long enough to double my striking distance without feeling cumbersome or difficult to control.

This wasn't made for a sport or as part of some costume.

131

This was a real weapon of war, used by real warriors. I remembered the story of Lady Hangaku, who wielded a naginata as she led three thousand soldiers to defeat an attacking army of ten thousand. Now this one was mine, and I was really supposed to use it to slice, stab, hook and beat my enemies. I shuddered, and held on tighter to the handle, steadying myself against this new and utterly bizarre reality I'd found myself adrift in.

I gave Sebastian a suspicious look. 'Where did this *come* from? Is this one of the things from Isobel's secret stash?'

'Ask me no questions and I'll tell you no lies,' said Sebastian, with a hint of a smug smile.

'*Seb*, where did you get this? And before you lie to me, let me remind you who's holding the big sharp pointy thing.'

'Well ...' Sebastian had the decency to look slightly sheepish. 'I may have ... liberated it from a museum.'

'You *stole* it?' I blinked, suddenly looking at the foppish, bitter, love-struck Hunter boy with entirely new eyes. 'You?'

'I specialise in destabilising security systems and finding workarounds for internal alarm triggers,' Sebastian said.

'So, you hacked into the museum and stole a priceless artefact,' I translated. 'I mean ... OK, but why?'

'It's traditional.' Sebastian shrugged. 'New Demon Hunters always use an old weapon. It's a tie to history. It's important.'

'And you did that for me? Even though you thought I was going to bail on you?'

He hunched his shoulders, defensively, as if he didn't want me to get any wild ideas about him not completely hating me or anything.

I smiled. *I see right through you, Sebastian, right to your soft, squishy core.*

'Wow,' I said. 'You're like a nerdy super-villain.'

'Told you he was a bad influence,' said Vesta. 'Can we get on with this, please, only I'm going to get consumption and die if we hang about in the rain on the crags in the middle of the night, and I don't want to die of highland romance clichés.'

'One of us'll have to pull through,' Minerva said, brushing the wet ropes of her hair out of her face and rather pointlessly wringing them out. 'They never kill off both twins.'

'I swear, the stuff they just keep in *boxes* in that museum,' Sebastian muttered, standing back. 'They'll take years to even notice it's gone.'

'All right,' Minerva said, raising her voice as the rain suddenly battered down harder, slamming into the rock. 'Di, V, you stay where you are, I'll find the third point.'

A roll of thunder above me made me shudder. I was going to be glad to have this done, and not just for spiritual destiny reasons – water was soaking through my jeans, seeping down through the thick woollen fabric of my jacket and running down the back of my neck. My hair had finally given up the struggle and lay down flat against the top of my head, and I was intensely grateful to past-me for wearing the sensible boots with the high tops that were keeping my feet relatively dry.

Lightning split the sky right above us with a roar of thunder louder than I'd ever heard, and I jumped and let out a high-pitched yelp. On my right, Vesta turned her face to the sky and giggled like a maniac, her silver sickle glinting as she spun it one-handed. In front of us, Minerva barely blinked, her attention flitting between Vesta and me and the uneven ground.

A visceral, terrifying moment of panic struck me, despite what I'd told Sebastian, despite that I was not my mother and I could *handle* this. I trembled with the urge to turn and

133

run. What was I doing? I was standing on a mountain, in the rain, holding a sword, with people I didn't know, preparing to pledge my life to them, for ever. And for what? To fight some demon that had killed some people I'd never met? To get some kind of revenge on a creature who'd pretended to want to date me?

Then Minerva found the right spot, and I knew that this was where I was meant to be. Power surged through me, more than before, almost too much. It juddered through me, just about on the right side of pain. My skin tingled.

'Ready?' Minerva yelled.

'Ready!' Vesta and I replied, as one.

My arm lifted, without me telling it to, and I found myself watching in exhilarated puzzlement as I held out the naginata, razor-sharp blade horizontal, splitting the raindrops.

I couldn't imagine why I'd been worried. I was a Demon Hunter. My blood *fizzed* with it. Everything else was up for discussion, but not this. The twins' arms had moved too, and now the crossbow and the sickle were pointing towards the same spot, the imaginary central point of our mystical triangle.

'Look!' Sebastian yelled, pointing upwards into the roiling clouds, his glassless glasses forgotten in his hand. It was an effort to look away from the middle of our triangle, but I dragged my gaze up, and saw ...

I didn't know what the hell it was. Something in the clouds, a giant shape, like a crack or a tear, hanging in the sky right over our heads. The rain in my eyes was almost blinding, but I could see that the shape was dark, and edged with glowing, unnatural colours.

Lightning crackled out of it and hit the ground, right in the middle of the triangle. It arced between our weapons and I couldn't help but squeeze my eyes shut as it leaped for me, filling my vision with white even behind my eyelids. For a second I braced for the pain of a million volts searing through me, but all I felt was a warm, energised feeling. It was just me and the twins, hanging suspended in a white void – my eyes were firmly closed, but I could feel them there.

We were blood. We were the same now.

The light went out, my whole body juddered as I came back down to earth with an almighty bump.

I opened my eyes slowly and raised my head. Then the wind and the rain and the darkness hit me all at once and I staggered, planting the handle of the naginata on the rocks in front of me so as not to fall flat on my face.

I looked up at the clouds, but they were already dispersing, the rain slowing. I wiped the water from my eyes and tried to find the strange tear in the sky, but it was gone – or maybe I just couldn't see it any more.

'Guys?' I said weakly, looking back at the twins. They were both standing like puppets with their strings cut, arms limp at their sides, heads slumped on their chests. Slowly, they blinked their eyes open and looked up at me, and at each other.

'Wow,' Vesta gasped, and dropped to her knees. A muddy, cream-coloured shape scrambled across the summit in front of me as Sebastian rushed to her side. Minerva wobbled, but managed to stay standing, and then walk, as both of us staggered over to Vesta.

'V?' Minerva said. 'You good?'

'Am I good? Are you having a laugh?' Vesta leaned hard on Sebastian's shoulder – he winced – and got back to her feet, light dancing in her eyes. 'That was amazing!'

I smiled, relieved, and reached up to push the tangle of wet hair back from my forehead. And suddenly, I realised that I was having a sensation ... or rather a lack of sensation. My

135

wrist had stopped itching. I tugged my sleeve up and stared down at my soaked skin with a shuddering gasp. Where there had been a red, angry rash, the skin was completely clear, but marked with a bright purple symbol, like a triangle in front of a group of interlocking circles. The colour was so vibrant it almost seemed to glow, even in the stormy pre-dawn murk.

'Thank God,' Minerva said, exposing her wrist to show us her identical mark. Vesta raised her arm too. 'I was so *tired* of the itching!'

I stared down at the mark, a mildly hysterical giggle rising in my throat. 'Wow ... I don't know how I'm going to explain this to my dad,' I said. *Yes, I had a great time with my new friends, oh and we all got matching tattoos on a whim ...*

'Come on, let's get back to the car and get dry,' Sebastian said, reaching for the bag and stowing our weapons again. I found myself strangely reluctant to let go of the naginata, but obviously we couldn't exactly head back to the parking lot carrying priceless, stolen, offensive weapons.

Sebastian took the staff from me. In that moment, we were standing closer than we had since we got out of the car, and I tried out a smile – a little *told you so* smile, hopefully not too smug. He gave me a brief nod. I guessed that was as good as I was going to get, for now.

'I can't believe Isobel didn't tell us about that thing with the colours,' Vesta said, shouldering the bag again and starting down the hill, her arm linked in Minerva's.

'I didn't see any colours,' I said, frowning, and then I remembered. 'Well, I saw the thing in the sky and the weird edges, but I shut my eyes when the lightning hit.'

'Aw, what? Then you missed the best part!'

'What? What happened?'

'I ... I can't.' Vesta shook her head, speechless again. I looked to Minerva, but she just blinked and shrugged.

'Don't look at me,' Sebastian said, 'I was cowering at the time. I thought you were all going to be fried!'

'Well, it's done now,' said Vesta. She threw an arm around my shoulders and the other around Minerva, and dragged us both into a hard, wet hug. 'We're bonded now. We're blood.'

I shuddered a little at her echoing the exact thought I had had. But she was right. We were. And it made me happy, deep in my chest.

Whatever else happened, we three were one, and I grinned into the rain as we picked our way back down Arthur's Seat towards the road, and the future.

CHAPTER SIXTEEN

By the time we made it back to the car, the rain had stopped, because of course it had. I suspected the storm had rolled in especially for us, and wasn't sure whether to feel flattered, powerful, or just slightly annoyed. I found myself glaring up at the dissipating clouds and thinking, *There's such a thing as dry lightning, you know*.

Sebastian had towels in Ruby's trunk, and we stood around her hood and dried ourselves off as the sun peeked sheepishly over the horizon, making the wet hillside look lush and green. Even with my nap at Isobel's house, I was starting to long for my own bed.

I frowned, as a tinny fanfare started up from my pocket. I pulled out my phone, saw that it was Dad, and my skin crawled. Why was he calling me at this hour? Didn't he get my message?

In the second it took me to pick up and hold the phone to my ear, I'd imagined a parade of horrible things. Fire. Burglary. Heart attacks. Dad in the hospital. Millie dead.

'Hey, Dad,' I said, trying to stamp on those ideas before they could get completely out of control.

For a moment, there was no noise except for a faint gurgling sound.

'Dad?' I said again, fear burning the back of my throat.

'Diana ...' Dad's voice was a cracked whisper. 'Diana, I was wrong ...'

'What? Dad, where are you? What's happening?'

'I love you, darling,' Dad said in a rush, and then there was a fleshy thump and a groan, and I gripped the phone so tight my hand shook. 'He wants me to tell you to come here. But don't come, understand?' He made that sound again and I flinched.

'Dad, please, I don't understand ...'

At the other end of the phone there was a rushing, rattling noise as if it was being taken, moved through the air, swapped from hand to hand. Then Dad's voice, yelling, but far away from the mic. 'Call the police, please, help me, but don't come to the graveyard! You understand? Don't come for me ...'

There was another thud, a gargling scream, and the call cut out. I couldn't move. Couldn't even lower the phone.

'Di? Di, what's happened?'

I felt my fingers gently prised apart as Vesta took the phone and stared at it.

'Diana,' Minerva said urgently, 'your father was investigating the museum ...'

I thought I had time to stop him. I thought I had time.

Vesta swore under her breath. 'Did he go there?'

I swallowed and shook my head. 'Graveyard. He said don't come to the graveyard. I don't even know where ...'

'Greyfriars,' Vesta said. I was vaguely aware of Sebastian gathering the towels and throwing them into the car. 'It's right by the museum.'

139

Minerva gripped my arms tight and spun me to face her. 'Listen to me. It's going to be all right. We're going to get him back.'

Vesta was already on the phone. She flicked it to speakerphone and rested it on the trunk of the car. It rang twice, then Isobel's voice said: 'Vesta? Is everything all right?'

'No,' Vesta said, and I tried to take a breath, and my chest hitched painfully. 'It's Diana's dad. He's at Greyfriars, Kincaid's got him. What do we do?'

Isobel didn't reply for a second.

'We bonded,' Minerva added. 'We can do this. Maybe we can get him and get out.'

'No,' said Isobel.

I stared at the phone, and then at the twins, confused.

'What does she ... What do you mean *no*?' I stammered, bracing my hands on the trunk to lean over the phone, my voice breaking on the words.

There was a silence that seemed to ring in my ears.

'You have to leave him,' Isobel said. 'Listen to me, Diana – it's a trap, there's nothing you can do. Your father is already dead.'

I stared down at the phone, rain still dripping from my hair on to the screen, unable to actually believe what I was hearing.

'You're not ready to face Kincaid; he will kill you. I'm sorry, but you're a Demon Hunter now, and you have to think of more than your own happiness. Come home. That's an order.'

My own happiness? I thought I was going to throw up. I couldn't make the words come out loud, but inside I was a shrieking mess. *My happiness? This is my father's life, this is real! You didn't hear the sounds he made ...*

'You can't mean that,' said Vesta, low and hollow. 'Aunt Isobel, it's her *Da*, we can't.'

'Diana, you can't save him. Come back to the house. I'll train you up and keep you safe, and then we will all get our revenge, I swear it.'

An icy calm came over me and I nodded. 'OK. Thank you for the advice,' I said. 'I'm going to go save my dad now.'

'No!' Isobel's shout overloaded the phone's speakers and came out as a distorted howl. 'Girls, are you listening to me? Put her in the car and bring her home, right—'

I hung up on her. Then I looked up at Minerva and Vesta, my eyes asking the question my tongue couldn't bear to put into words.

'No, screw that,' Vesta said, and I tried not to visibly sag with the relief. 'What is she thinking? We're with you, Di, no matter what.'

Minerva glanced at Sebastian. 'What about you, Seb? You in, or are we going to have to walk up to Greyfriars?'

Sebastian was chewing his thumbnail, shivering. 'Jesus,' he said. 'We're all going to regret this. Get in, quick.'

Minerva steered me into Ruby's back seat and then jumped into the front. Sebastian had the engine running, and he put his foot down before Minerva's door was even all the way shut. We roared out of the silent parking lot and the panic came back with a vengeance.

This was insane. This couldn't be real, it was just some new and horrifying nightmare. I just had to find a way to wake up.

I clutched the door handle for balance, and the metal was cold and slightly damp under my hand. I focused on the feeling of my wet jeans drying out against my skin, and gradually the reality of the sensation battered its way into my mind. I tried to pull myself together.

'It's a trap,' Vesta said, grabbing my free hand and giving it a squeeze. 'Of course it is. But he doesn't know what we know, does he?' I frowned at her, trying to think what I knew that could possibly help me right now. 'You're a Demon Hunter! You're more powerful than he could ever understand.'

I couldn't really believe her, but I brightened anyway, thinking of Vesta's strength and Minerva's blasts of ice-white fire, and my own power – unpredictable as it was. Vesta's arm slung around my neck and she pulled me into a damp, fierce hug.

'We're going to get him back,' she said, and held on tight until I'd stopped shaking.

Sebastian swerved around a corner and Ruby's suspension rattled underneath us as we charged over a cobbled road and skidded around a roundabout, throwing Vesta and me against the back seat as we climbed a steep hill. I grabbed on even harder to the door handle as I realised we were barrelling the wrong way up a deserted one-way street, and then we slipped down an alley behind the museum and came to a halt, haphazardly half-hidden behind a stack of wooden pallets.

We tumbled out of the car and Vesta opened the trunk and shouldered the bag of weapons. Minerva squeezed my arm and held her finger to her lips. I nodded. It was still early, and for now the street was deserted, but there was no sense drawing attention to ourselves.

She led the way across the road, past a row of darkened shops. The National Museum of Scotland loomed behind us with its faux-medieval tower in clean, pale brick, but the entrance to Greyfriars Kirkyard was unassuming, tall iron gates standing in a small gap between an art supply store and a pub.

The pub was named Greyfriars Bobby, after the dog that

legend said had sat by his master's grave in the churchyard for fourteen years. There was an iron statue of the dog on a post just outside the pub. It was a sweet little Skye terrier.

This was all so surreal. But Dad's voice had been real. His cry for help had been real. And the lightning and surge of power and the hole in the sky ... that had been real, too.

Beyond the gate, a pretty medieval church sat in well-kept grass, surrounded by gravestones.

The gate was shut with a heavy chain, but Vesta stepped forwards and flexed her fingers, then carefully twisted and pulled until the links split and gave way. It didn't seem like her first time. Neither she nor Minerva seemed especially fazed by the idea of breaking into a church at half past four in the morning, either – I couldn't help wondering if they had done this kind of thing a lot in their years of training.

Vesta paused to catch her breath before she quietly unthreaded the chain and eased the gate open. Minerva slipped inside, and then I followed. Vesta paused and held up her hand in front of Sebastian's face.

'But—' Sebastian started to say.

'No.' Vesta gave him a gentle shove that sent him staggering backwards, and closed the gate between them. 'It's not safe. Stay by the car and keep a lookout.' She backed away. 'Stay. Good boy,' she added, with a teasing smile.

'Be careful,' Sebastian mouthed to us, his hands closing around the iron bars of the gate.

I looked around, a deep unease threatening to turn back into panic as I took in the pretty church, the grass, the graves, the cool early-morning light, and found absolutely nothing that seemed out of the ordinary. No demons. No Dad.

You're here somewhere, I thought. *And if Kincaid is too, so much the better. I've got an ancient Japanese sword-staff with his name on it.*

We skirted close around the edge of the church. The largest part of the graveyard sloped downhill, a smooth incline dotted with standing tombstones and lined around the edges with individual plots. Some of them were moss-covered and crumbling, others had clean lines of brick around them and names engraved in bright gold on elaborate headstones as tall and wide as Sebastian's car.

At the bottom of the hill, through the leaves of tall trees, I could see the Edinburgh skyline looming – the castle on its ledge of rock, sloping roofs layered up one behind the other, and the elaborate, pointed towers of churches. It was so beautiful. How could such a wonderful place harbour demons?

We paused every few steps, but nothing moved in the graveyard except for a few early birds. I laid my palm against the cold stone of the church, hoping for ... I wasn't sure what, perhaps for the church to remember what had happened here. But there was nothing.

We had nearly gone all the way around the church, and I was starting to think we were going to have to break into it, when I saw a something move. Something man-shaped.

I grabbed at the twins, mostly to stop them from walking out where he could see them, but partly to steady myself against the shuddering. It was Alex.

I looked up at him, and thought I might be sick. He looked so normal. Still beautiful, yes, but *human*, like he could grow stubble and get pimples and split his lip if he fell. His blue shirt was crumpled. It was the same one he'd been wearing on our date. His hands and forearms were smeared with dirt. I was sure I didn't want to know why. He turned to glance around, and I caught my breath, but he didn't see us. He approached the corner of the graveyard. I peered through the trees and saw there was another iron gate, and squat square mausoleums beyond.

'That's the Covenanters' Prison,' Minerva whispered, as he pulled open the gate and slipped through.

I gave her a shaken *the what?* look. That sounded bad. I wasn't sure what Covenanters were, but I'd watched enough horror movies to know that an ancient prison *inside a graveyard* had to be very bad news.

'They kept political prisoners there,' Minerva explained, entirely confirming my bad feeling about the place. 'Hundreds died. It's supposed to be incredibly haunted, but I thought we'd never found any demon activity.'

'Well, there's our demon activity right there,' Vesta hissed. 'He'll lead us to Kincaid – if we don't let him get away.' She slipped out from our relatively safe spot at the corner of the church and hurried across the damp green lawn towards the black gate. I clenched my fists and forced myself to follow her. One foot in front of the other, that was all I needed to do. Just keep going.

Vesta sidled up to the wall beside the gate and peered through, then waved Minerva and me over. 'He slipped into a gap between two of the mausoleums. There must be something behind there.'

I swallowed hard. 'I guess now's not a good time to mention I hate small spaces.'

Vesta gave my shoulder a reassuring squeeze and smiled sympathetically, before saying, 'Not remotely, no.'

We entered the Covenanters' Prison and trod carefully down the grassy avenue, along the rows of the dead, to the gap where Vesta had seen Alex disappear. I peered into the dim gap with my heart in my mouth, half expecting him to lunge out and grab me. But there was nobody there.

Vesta put down the weapons bag, and opened it up. I looked around. For a moment, I was genuinely nervous that we were going to get caught in this public place with some very offensive, very stolen weapons. Then I realised that that was a stupid way to feel: I *ought* to be scared that we were about to go somewhere we might need to *use* them. I gripped the handle of the naginata so tight my knuckles stood out white against my skin.

I let Vesta go first into the gap, but then I followed her, walking sideways, my free hand out to feel my way along the stone mausoleum wall. I felt a twist of sick panic in my stomach, and the nonsensical urge to pound uselessly on the stone wall with my bare fists, just because it was so *in my way*. But I forced myself to go on, muttering to myself, 'Suck it up, Helsing. It's not even dark.'

Vesta reached the back of the low building, and peered around the corner. 'Ah,' she said.

'What?' Minerva hissed. 'What now?'

'Down,' Vesta said. She stepped out into a space just barely wide enough for us to walk straight, and I looked around the corner to find a hidden flight of stone steps that vanished into the earth, and into darkness.

Great.

Vesta wriggled, pulled her cellphone out of her jeans and switched on its torch. Minerva and I did the same, and followed her down.

The steps weren't like the grand, shabby headstones or mausoleums in the graveyard – there was no intricate Victorian Gothic architecture going on here. They actually looked as if stones from a wall somewhere had been unceremoniously driven down into the earth. I tried not to look up at the roof when I passed underneath it and into the dark passage beyond, but I couldn't help noticing that there wasn't much holding it up.

When we reached the bottom, Vesta raised her phone and swung it around so that we could see what we were dealing with. The passage curved to the right, still only just wide enough for us to walk down without brushing our shoulders against the damp stone walls. I was reminded of the cold, black chamber that Alex had pushed me into. Could this be the other end of those tunnels? Could they run all over the city, under the ground?

'Heeere, demon, demon, demon,' Vesta said, and stepped forward, sickle held out in front of her.

Our footsteps sounded strange on the smooth cobbles underfoot, and I pointed my light down at my feet. Something about the way some of the stones had splintered and decayed was very wrong. They were the wrong colour, as well. Too white, or too yellow.

I swallowed, and nudged one of the 'stones' with my toe. It came away from the ground quite easily, and rolled over to reveal a pattern of cracks, spurs and rough textures that was eerily familiar.

'It's bones,' I whispered. The twins both looked down and shuddered, taking in identical stifled breaths.

'From the graveyard?' Minerva hazarded. Neither Vesta nor I replied, but I wondered if we were thinking the same thing – *Oh God, I hope so.*

On any other day, Dad would love this, I thought, with a sick twist in my stomach. *He should be down here with his instruments, taking readings, talking to the walls. Not kidnapped and beaten. Not dead.*

I'm coming for you, Dad. I'm going to get you out of this horrible place.

The passage straightened out, which I would have said was a good thing, until Vesta stepped aside to let us peer past her. She raised her torch and its beam illuminated about ten metres of corridor and, much further down, in the darkness, there was a doorway. Beyond it, I could see a soft and flickering yellow light.

The memory that this was almost certainly a trap struck me hard and I reached out and stopped Vesta from walking forward. Her strength would be invaluable in a fight, but it wouldn't be much good to us if we set off some kind of Indiana Jones nonsense and she was impaled or burned up or something before the fighting even started.

'I should go first,' I mouthed, hefting the long naginata and holding it out in front of me, demonstrating how much further its reach could go. Its sharp cutting edge flared in the light from Minerva's phone.

'Sure?' Vesta asked.

I really, really wasn't sure. But I nodded anyway, and squeezed by her. Our torch lights danced and flashed around the walls. Anyone in the room beyond the doorway would know we were coming, but it was better than fumbling in the dark.

I stepped forward, my heart in my mouth, but feeling much braver now that I had the unsheathed sword end of the naginata held out in front of me, almost at its full reach. I swept it around at head, waist and knee height, and then across the floor, holding on tight in case some hand reached out of a corner I couldn't see and tried to grab it. But there was nothing I could feel waiting to spring, and no sound but the scrape of the blade across the stone.

I changed my grip slightly, for more control – anyone who ran at me would meet the tip of my blade before they got within grabbing distance. Then I stepped inside, flashing my torch all around, looking for telltale signs of movement.

There was no demonic attacker waiting in the darkness for us. Instead, there were heads.

Hundreds of heads.

The room was large and lofty, with a vaulted stone ceiling. The flickering light was coming from candles set in sconces around the walls. Moss crawled over the floor and the walls and dripped from the stone up above.

But it was the heads that commanded the attention.

The walls were covered in catacombs, but instead of the drawers holding whole bodies with nice thick slabs over the top, they were all open, and there were heads sitting at the mouth of each one. Some were ancient, dried-out skulls. Those were the least frightening. It was the ones that still had skin stretched thinly across their faces that forced a whimper from my lips.

Some of them were desiccated, yellow teeth jutting out from broken jaws. Some had been broken before they'd been severed. Smashed cheekbones, smashed noses, ripped skin that shrank away from the lips and wrinkled as it dried. Some still had hair that hung in nasty ropes from their scalps. All the hair was long. A few, sickeningly, were recent enough that their eyeballs were shrivelled and dried but still intact inside their sockets. I wondered, distantly, if I would throw up.

The twins stepped into the room behind me, and I heard their breathing speed up. One of them made a quiet retching sound, but I wasn't sure which.

'Oh no ... no,' Minerva whispered. 'It's not ...'

'It is. Look, look at the labels.' Vesta's voice was low and shaking with anger.

I hadn't noticed the labels, but I saw them now. Yellowing strips of paper, scrawled with handwriting that I knew all too well. It was still etched into the back of my closet, back at home.

Mary the priest's wife, one said. *Patricia the healer. Kathryn the epicurist. Jeanne the blacksmith's daughter.*

If I'd been in any doubt that they were all women, I wasn't any more.

'Kincaid's victims?' I managed, glancing back at Minerva. She nodded. There were tears in her eyes, and I looked away. I felt like I might vomit, but I didn't feel like crying any more. I just felt like ...

'They're not all ancient,' Vesta said, her voice choked. 'Look at them. Some of these women died ... *recently*.'

My hands tightened on the naginata, all hesitation fleeing from my heart. Right now, I felt like killing something.

I tried to think practically, and I was about to say that there must be another way out, because we hadn't passed Alex and he wasn't anywhere in the room, when I noticed one of the catacombs on the other side of the room was labelled but empty.

'That must be where he got the head he left in the museum,' I muttered, and started towards it to read the label.

Then there was a sound like stone dragging across stone, and I spun around, afraid I'd see the doorway we'd come in through close behind us. But the twins' horrified gazes were fixed on an alcove on the other side of the room, and I found it just in time to see the stones moving, as if they had a life of their own, the wall peeling back to reveal another corridor.

Behind the wall, held down to an ancient-looking wooden chair with straps made of old and flaking leather, was my dad. He was gagged. His glasses were knocked sideways on his face, and there was a huge mottled streak of purple and yellow across his cheekbone and chin, which took me a second to even realise was a bruise.

'Dad!' I screamed, all pretence of stealth forgotten, and launched myself across the room to claw at the leather straps. 'Dad, I'm here, it's going to be OK.'

'Nmhmmm! Hm!' He shook his head and looked up at me, his eyes wider and darker than I'd ever seen them.

Then something lifted me off my feet and threw me back.

150

I felt like a twanging razor-sharp wire had cut through my body from my knees to the top of my head. I heard myself scream, and then the floor came up to meet me and knocked the breath from my lungs. I felt a bone in my shoulder crunch and I choked, because I couldn't gasp.

Strong hands gripped me tight and tugged me backwards across the slimy flagstones. I couldn't breathe. I fought not to panic.

'You're all right,' said Vesta's voice somewhere above me. 'Just winded. Stay here.' I realised she'd dragged me to the side of the room and propped me up against the wall. I blinked, focusing on her face. 'It's OK, just stay down,' she said, and turned away, joining Minerva as she stood in front of me.

I took short, fast breaths and my swimming vision focused again slowly. Minerva's crossbow was unfolded, a bolt already notched to the string. Vesta's sickle gleamed in the candlelight. The naginata had clattered from my hand and was lying nearby, not quite in reach.

Dad was still in the chair. And coming out of the shadows behind him, two figures.

One of them was Alex. I swallowed and glared at him, feeling the queasy pull and push of attraction and repulsion.

I wanted him to look at me, so that he would know how much I hated him. But he didn't even glance down towards me – his eyes were fixed on the twins.

Unlike Alex's poised stride, the other man's gait was strange and his shoulders were hunched. He stepped into the light, a dark cloak of rough-weaved material hiding most of his body and sweeping around his feet. It was shiny with grease and dirt, and pockmarked with little holes. *Motheaten*, I realised, feeling sick.

His face was twisted up into a sneer, made lopsided by a

wide, ragged scar that tugged down one side from his eye to his chin. His skin was a patchwork of sagging wrinkles, crusted scabs and scar tissue. Long, greasy hair clung to his scalp and hung down to his chin.

'And here they are,' he whispered, and his voice was thick and bubbled horribly in his throat. It was the same voice I'd heard in the dark chamber. 'The three lost little girls.'

'We're not lost,' Minerva said. 'We're here to destroy you.'

He flung back the folds of his cloak and his hands came out, holding another head.

'You have served my purposes once more by bringing them to me,' he said, lifting and turning the head to speak to her face. 'Time for you to get back in your place.' He placed the head back into its empty catacomb, caressing its cheek with one hand. 'Elspeth, the Whore.'

Elspeth. Isobel's friend. My ancestor. It was her head he left by the Maiden. I struggled to get to my knees and reached for the naginata. I may not have powers like the twins, but I wasn't just going to lie on the floor while they handled this for me.

Vesta stepped forward, her sickle raised, but the man moved like an oily snake and grabbed Dad's head. He twisted. Dad let out a muffled scream. Vesta hesitated, her hand clenching on the handle of the weapon.

I seized the sword and leaped to my feet. My head spun and I was paralysed for a second, leaning heavily on the handle of the naginata. The tone of Dad's voice turned angry and I could tell he was swearing underneath his gag. Kincaid slapped him hard. I stepped between Minerva and Vesta, hefting the naginata, ready to plunge its tip into the man's heart. But their hands grabbed my elbows, holding me tight.

'Ah, there you are.' The man smiled, and I got a glimpse of brown and yellow teeth. 'Diana Helsing. The lost Fleming. At long last.'

'He'll kill you,' Minerva whispered. 'That's what he wants.'

'Get away from her,' the man snarled, and lifted his clenched fists. 'She's mine!'

This time I saw the shock wave coming. It was like a thin line of heat haze, as if the man had twisted the world and sent a ripple of energy and wrongness shooting towards us. The twins' arms tightened on mine as the wave hit. The razor-wire cut through me at chest height and I staggered, letting out an involuntary *oof!* But the twins had braced for it, and somehow the three of us managed to stay standing.

'Get away, Gowdie's spawn!' The man reached into his cloak again and pulled out something long, thin and dark. It was a whip. It twisted at his feet, and then with an easy flick of his wrist he sent it slicing through the air towards us.

We sprang apart, and the spiked end of the whip slashed down where Minerva's arm had been.

'How rude of me,' the man gurgled. 'I have not yet introduced myself. I am John Kincaid.'

CHAPTER SEVENTEEN

I glared into the twisted, ruined face of the hunched man.

'No freaking kidding,' I snapped.

Kincaid's eyes widened.

'You're John Kincaid, the Witch Pricker. We know. Old-ass serial killer. Big freaking whoop. I . . . *demand* you release my father!' The tremble in my voice was surely giving me away, showing my bravado for what it really was – simple terror. But Kincaid's split lip twisted in an angry snarl and he cracked the whip again. All three of us shrank back, drifting further apart.

'How dare you say such things to me?' he hissed.

I wasn't sure how I dared, to be honest. My hands twisted on the handle of the naginata, slick with sweat. I longed to lash out and stab it into the heart of the foul old man who had killed all of these women and kidnapped my father. But I guessed that if I did, all I'd achieve would be another shock wave and a cracked skull on the old stones behind me.

I looked into Dad's eyes – they were almost black, his

pupils huge with terror – and then up at the boy who was standing behind him, the one I'd had been foolish enough to think might be my friend.

'What are you really, Alex?' I snapped, doing my best to ignore the furious face of the Witch Pricker. 'Are you even really a person?'

Alex didn't reply, but Kincaid's anger melted into a horrible grin, yellow and black teeth dimly visible behind his cracked and wrinkled lips.

'Yes, you two have met, have you not?' said Kincaid, his voice as oily as his ratty grey hair. 'Alexander is my friend, he has been helping me.'

Alex's expression was dully angry, staring at the floor as if he was the one who had been betrayed. He couldn't even meet my eyes.

'Diana Helsing.' Kincaid ran the whip through his fingers, caressing it. 'I have been waiting for you. The hawkmoths, the harbingers of death – they brought you to me, in your dreams. They have already shown you what awaits you.'

'The only death your disgusting insects are harbingers of is yours,' I babbled, trying not to think of the needles and knives in my nightmares. I wished Minerva and Vesta were still holding me back – they'd moved away from me now towards the sides of the room. Kincaid wasn't even looking at them; his nasty yellow weeping eyes were fixed on me. I was free, but I just felt alone.

I glanced at Alex again. 'Come on, Alex. This is messed up, and you know it if any part of you is still human. Let my dad go!'

Kincaid threw a glance over his shoulder. Alex flinched as if he'd been struck. Then his lips twitched into a sneer.

'Pathetic, gullible girl,' he said. The words sounded wrong in his voice. 'It was so easy to make you follow me here.' He spat on the ground by Dad's foot. I felt my scalp prickle with disgust.

Fine. He's not who I thought he was. He's not anybody. 'We came here on purpose,' I snarled at Kincaid. 'We knew this was your plan.'

'And still you came to me, Helsing. Last of a long line who have evaded my grasp, you come to me because you know your destiny is waiting for you at the Maiden.' Kincaid's voice seemed to crawl under my skin and settle there, wriggling like his precious moths. But while he was talking to me, he wasn't looking to either side. I spotted Minerva first, her blonde hair catching the light before melting back into the shadows. And yes, Vesta was there too. They were moving with purpose, like they had a plan.

I tried not to let the relief show on my face. I had to keep Kincaid's attention.

'I came to get my father back,' I said. I had a brainwave and let the naginata clatter to the floor beside me. 'I don't want to fight you. I don't know what kind of beef you had with my ancestors but it's got nothing to do with me. What do you want? I'll do anything!'

Kincaid's eyes gleamed in the yellow torchlight.

Gotcha. I had his full attention now. His lips peeled back in another broken grin. I felt like I could shower for years and never feel clean again, but as long as it bought the twins enough time to get to Dad, or take out Alex . . .

I risked a glance up. The twins were still edging away from me. Alex was standing behind Dad's chair, his knuckles white on the wood, so still I couldn't see him breathing. Maybe he wasn't. He looked like a dead thing, or a robot that was waiting for its next command.

I refocused on Kincaid.

'I don't want any of this!' I wailed. 'I don't know what

156

the hell's going on. I'm not special, I'm not powerful, I just wanted to go to a party!' I raised my voice to a high-pitched whine. 'I will do anything you want,' I repeated. 'Just let my daddy go.'

I thought 'daddy' might be too much, but Kincaid looked like I'd made his day. He held up a hand and crooked a finger.

'Come closer,' he said. 'Come to me, sweet Diana, and say that again.'

Crap. I didn't want to get a single inch closer to that walking corpse, not when he was looking at me like he was a cat and I was a fat, sleepy little mouse. But I didn't have a choice. I forced myself to take a slow step forwards, into the circle of flickering light around the hidden door. He beckoned again, the cracked yellow nail on the end of his finger carving through the air. I swallowed and took another step.

Something bright purple flashed in the dark crevices of the tomb, drawing my eye before I could stop myself. It was like a twist of neon hanging in the air, leaving strange after-effects where it raised up and—

I felt my wrist tingling and looked down. My mark was glowing, the same violent purple.

Minerva's voice rang out from the darkness, crying out in Gaelic. Lightning flickered around her hands, gathering between her fingertips, but she didn't let fly yet. Kincaid spun around, and I took the only opportunity I thought I was going to get, twisting and planting a swift and heavy kick square in the middle of his back. He staggered – but by rights he should've gone down on to his knees. Instead, he recovered with an angry gasp and flung up his hands.

The burst of energy distorted the world all around it. Minerva was still chanting when it hit her and her voice cut off in a high-pitched shriek as she was borne backwards, clattering into a shelf and sending skulls crashing and rattling to the floor.

'Don't think you can lure me out, witch!' Kincaid screamed. 'This body is mine, this work is *mine*. This is what happens to women who try to challenge me!' He scooped up a skull that had rolled towards him and held it up, his fingers hooked into its eye sockets. 'Even your precious Elspeth – she may have evaded my blade, but she couldn't hide from me once she was in her grave.'

While I was staring, still processing that bit of information, he twisted and hurled the skull towards the purple glow where Vesta was standing. She arced her fist around to meet it, the mark leaving a trailing purple after-image in the air. The skull shattered.

'Diana, do not move!' she yelled. I froze, realising what they planned to do, but my instincts still screaming at me to *get him*. Kincaid was a few steps from me. I could have ducked back to grab the naginata, or forward to try to grab him into a joint lock … 'Di, I mean it, stay there! Min?'

'I'm here,' said Minerva faintly. 'Hurry, V.'

Vesta stepped forwards, dancing lightly across the floor, glancing at me, then Minerva, then me, judging the distance.

I felt it, when she found the spot – the surge of power started in my wrist and then shot through my veins and into my heart, my brain, my spine and stomach. The world *fizzed*.

The feeling balled in my throat. I had to let it out. I opened my mouth and it shot out of me as an involuntary, joyful laugh.

'No!' Kincaid screeched and threw out his fists.

I saw the wave of energy burst from his palms and sweep towards all three of us. I planted my feet, but when it hit, I felt nothing.

Kincaid, Alex, the chair, my dad – they were all caught up in our invisible net.

The rush of power was intense, like a super-charged burst of endorphins from victory in a ju-jitsu tournament, and it was all the more incredible for knowing that he was trapped. We had him.

Vesta and Minerva raised their hands, the mark standing out brighter than ever. I matched them with my own.

'You can't ...' Kincaid couldn't finish his sentence. He was trembling. He backed away, hobbling worse than before, and tried to throw himself out of the triangle, but he couldn't do it. He recoiled from the boundary with a wince and a cry. He spun around, facing me now, and ...

My whole body seemed to go cold, the power flowing now more like ice than fire in my veins.

Kincaid's face was crumpling into slack folds that hung loosely from his skull. Thick, dark globs of blackness seeped from the gap between his skin and muscle, out of his eyes, his ears, his nose. It took me a second to realise that it was old, congealed blood. It streaked his face, pooling and running in sticky rivulets.

'Oh my God!' I cried out. I thought I was going to be sick.

'Courage, Di!' Minerva said. 'Hold on, just a little longer!'

I looked over at Alex, fearing that I'd see the same terrible transformation happening to him, but his face hadn't changed.

Kincaid raised a hand to wipe the blood from his eyes, and something thick and yellow fell and bounced on the stones at his feet – it was one of his fingernails.

'Witches,' he muttered, his speech slurred but the hatefulness coming through loud and clear. 'Filthy devil women, you can't ... can't stop me. I will never stop, never, until all your kind are dead.'

Demon Hunters, or just girls in general? I thought, a little hysterically. I glanced at Alex again and found him watching his master disintegrate with a desperate light in his eyes. But he didn't move to help him.

'*Helsing*,' Kincaid whispered, and turned to fix his bloody eyes on me. 'You think you are a Demon Hunter? You are no Hunter, you are nothing. I cannot be destroyed. My bond to this body is too strong. I have kept it alive for centuries.'

I shuddered. He must be lying to us, trying to distract us. Right?

Clots of black blood dripped from his mouth and ears and splatted on the stones underfoot, but he was still standing.

'You can keep me in your net,' Kincaid chuckled. 'But will you do it? Will you stand by and watch your father die? Alexander, kill him!'

Alex's eyes turned dull and lifeless as his hands moved to Dad's throat. Dad gave a horrible muffled cry, then it cut off as Alex squeezed.

'No!' I yelled, and twitched to step forwards.

'Diana, don't move!' Minerva gasped. 'We have him, you have to hold the line!'

'I can't!' Dad's face was turning red as Alex's fingers went white with effort. Kincaid gave a bloody chuckle. The twins were both talking now, near-unison voices begging me to stand still. 'He's right, it isn't working! I can't, I *can't*!' I leaped towards Dad, breaking the alignment. I felt it go, felt the terrible lack of connection, but my fist was already balled and ready. It slammed into Alex's face and I used my full weight to bear him to the ground.

I tried to get right up, to get to Dad, but a burst of hot energy slammed into the back of my head and I went down again, cold stone on my cheek and stars flashing before my eyes.

160

Kincaid's laughter was high-pitched, triumphant and nasty.

I couldn't move, couldn't breathe, see or think. I heard flapping and rattling, footsteps scrambling on stone. I fought against the blackness that closed over me, tried to claw my way back to the surface, but then there was just a deep, cold nothing.

I snapped back with a gasp, tried to scramble to my feet and grab the naginata and thrust it into Kincaid's awful face ...

But Kincaid was gone. I spun around, half tripping on the blood-slick stones, sending two of the severed heads rolling. Alex was gone. Dad was gone.

So were Minerva and Vesta.

'V?' I called out. 'Min, please, don't be ... don't ...' But my voice faded. Nobody answered.

Kincaid had taken them.

The opening where he and Alex had appeared was gone, too. The stones of the wall had folded back into themselves, and the only sign that Kincaid had been here was a scrawled message written across the flat alcove wall. Written, I realised, in the same black and clotting blood that had been streaming from his eyes before I'd broken the line.

I have them all. Come to the Maiden. Come to your death.

Anger flared in my heart and I kicked the wall, letting out a wail of impotent fury. 'Come back!' My words rasped painfully but I screamed them out anyway, pounding on the wall. 'Come back here and face me, you demon coward!'

The air was full of ancient stone dust and the stink of blood. Red, sticky liquid and shards of shattered skull trailed cross the floor. But there was no reply from beyond the secret door.

The Witch Pricker was on the move, and he had my father. And now he had my sisters, too.

CHAPTER EIGHTEEN

Sebastian was still at the Greyfriars gate. He looked up hopefully as I staggered around the corner of the church, just as the clock on the tower struck 5 a.m. and the early morning stillness was split by an ominous peal of bells.

It almost physically hurt to watch him, his expression gradually shifting from hope to horror as he realised that I was alone, spattered with blood and dust, carrying the naginata in its bag slung over my shoulder.

'Diana?' he gasped. 'Diana, where are the twins? Where is Vesta? What happened? Diana?'

I didn't answer, couldn't, until I got to the gate and he let me out, his hands shaking.

'He took them,' I said, my voice still harsh and whispery. I swallowed. 'We couldn't destroy him, and he took them. Dad too. He has them.'

Sebastian looked like he might faint. 'Kincaid?' I nodded. 'Oh my God.'

I grabbed him by the sleeve and dragged him after me out

of the alley. The street was no longer completely deserted – a few cars and delivery vans sailed past us, hopefully too fast to see or care that I looked exactly as bad as I felt. I pointed across the road to the tall, pale brick building.

'He had a secret passageway. He's taken them in there. Into the museum. To the Maiden.'

Sebastian swore under his breath and sped up to match my pace.

'We're going to need your gentleman thief skills,' I said, staring up at the museum, realising I didn't have the faintest idea how we'd get inside. Sneaking into a public graveyard was all very well, but this was just straight-up breaking and entering.

'My laptop's in the car. It could take me ...' He shook his head. 'I'll get it done.'

We slipped across the road and down the back alley behind the museum where Ruby was parked. Sebastian threw himself into the back seat and had his laptop open in seconds. He started typing furiously. A faint, sensible voice at the back of my head told me I ought to sit down, that I'd only had a few hours' nap since yesterday morning and a minute's unconsciousness did not count, that inside this building, right behind this wall, a demon was waiting to kill me and I didn't have the faintest idea how I could defeat it.

But I just couldn't get in the car. I couldn't stop pacing, my hand clamped around my wrist as if I could transmit my thoughts through the mark to Minerva and Vesta. *Stay strong. Stay alive. I'm coming.*

'How?' Sebastian muttered, from the back seat. 'How did he get them and not you?'

I swallowed back a wave of guilt. If I hadn't broken the line, maybe Kincaid was lying, if I hadn't moved out of alignment we could have held him ...

'It's my fault,' I said. I glanced at Sebastian, caught the fury building behind his eyes, and cut him off. 'He was killing my dad right in front of my eyes. I'm saying it's my fault, but it's not up for discussion. There's no world in which I could ever have let that happen.'

Sebastian said nothing. He stared for a second, then went back to typing.

I still felt the guilt, but I tried to fold it up smaller and smaller until it was a tiny, compact thing inside me, fuelling the anger burning in my gut. This was all down to Kincaid, and the demon riding him. This man and his hellish, parasitic little friend had been murdering women for centuries, collecting their heads in that gruesome place. Forget Elspeth and Isobel, forget Demon Hunters for a second.

This was a serial killer, and he had my family. There was no world in which I wouldn't need to stop him.

'It's done,' Sebastian said, breaking into my panicked reverie as he unfolded himself out of the car and shut the door behind him.

'Already?' I said, giving him a stunned look. 'What kind of genius—' Then I saw the expression on his face. It was grim.

'It wasn't me,' he said. 'Someone's already done it. The whole security system, cameras, everything. It's been off since eight o'clock last night.'

'Kincaid,' I said. 'Right.'

'I think he's emptied the place,' said Sebastian, raking his fingers through his hair. 'No cleaners, no researchers, no security guards.'

'Of course, wouldn't want those pesky guards walking in while you're having a beheading,' I said, feeling hollow. 'So how do I get in?'

Sebastian fumbled in his pockets and pulled out an enormous bunch of keys. He flipped through them until he found one that looked, to me, almost exactly like the others. He held it tight, and swallowed nervously.

'We open the door with this. But I'm not going to tell you where the door is unless you promise you won't try to stop me coming with you.'

'Seb ...' I shook my head. 'You're not even a Demon Hunter. He's probably going to kill me – *you* he'll *eat alive*.'

'I still have to try. Please, I can't stand out here and wait. Not again. I won't.' He shook his head. 'You can't ask me to stand around not knowing if any of you are ever coming out again.'

I hesitated for a long moment. 'Don't get killed,' I said finally. 'If you die on me, I'm going to tell Vesta that you were in love with her.'

Sebastian managed to go even paler. 'That's low,' he muttered, and beckoned me to follow him further down the alley. I found myself smiling at the back of his head. Despite everything, I was glad to have him with me. Now probably wasn't the time to say it, but I really hoped that the two of them managed to get together – or, if Vesta wasn't interested, that he could find somebody who was.

He was leading us to a neat glass door that looked like a kind of back entrance reception, maybe somewhere the researchers and museum staff came in to work. I headed towards it, but then Sebastian made a nervous coughing noise.

'Um. Not that one. I couldn't get the keys for that one.'

'Then, where ...?' I turned, and saw that he was standing next to a tall wooden fence. Behind it, I could see there was a small space, and then the brick wall of the building.

'The way in is behind there.'

'So, climbing. Great.' I unshouldered the bag with the naginata, took a deep steadying breath, and then posted it

165

over the top of the fence. 'No going back now.' I shrugged, when Sebastian gave me a worried look.

I stood back and placed the toe of my boot on the surface of the fence. There was a cross-support at waist height that would make a fine toehold to lift me up and over the top, if I could just get my foot on to it. It took two jumps, a desperate scramble and a painfully broken fingernail, but I got my boot on to the plank and pushed until I was up and sitting on the top, wobbling a little. I clung on for dear life, risking a glance towards the end of the alley, and feeling my heart thump in my chest when I realised there were people passing by now. We were mostly obscured by Ruby and the pallets, but if someone looked right, at the wrong moment ...

I reached down and offered Sebastian my hand, and pulled him shakily up until he could boost himself on the bar and drop down on the other side.

'You did this by yourself? With a whole bag of looted weapons?' I panted.

'Only once,' Sebastian admitted. We leaned on the fence and caught our breath for a second. The door into the building was small, simple and painted white. Sebastian got out his key and fitted it into the lock. 'I'm not really a return-to-the-scene-of-the-crime kind of guy.'

The door swung open without a sound. We were in.

I took the naginata from its bag and held it defensively in front of me as I led the way into the museum. We were in a dim marble corridor with a low curved ceiling, hung with informative posters about Scottish history and lined with benches. I held my breath and listened hard for voices, footsteps, cries for help, but there were none. I glanced at a map of the museum that we passed, and felt my heart sink. This place was much bigger than I'd thought. Seven floors, including the roof terrace. There had to be twenty separate gallery rooms in here. And that was only the public stuff . . .

Even with the place deserted, would I hear Dad calling for me?

I tried not to let the thought paralyse me. I'd been told to come here, and I'd come. If I didn't find them by myself, Kincaid would eventually come looking for me, right?

It wasn't a comforting thought, but it certainly got me moving.

At the end of the corridor, bright daylight lit up a huge white room with vaunted archways around the walls. I stepped out into the light and looked up, amazed, at the enormous gallery. It was three or four storeys high, white-painted iron supporting balconies on every floor and a glass roof that let the early morning daylight stream down, illuminating a collection of artefacts that I deeply wished I could be interested in right now, and one I wished I could look away from.

There it was, right in front of me. The Maiden.

I'd seen it in the pictures Dad had shown me of where Elspeth's head had been found, but I hadn't understood how tall, how old, how black it was. I knew that its supports were ancient timber, but it gleamed in the daylight as I skirted it nervously, looking more like black iron, or some prehistoric fossil.

But it was clean. The white platform where it stood was still white, and not dripping red. I felt light-headed, as a weight lifted off me that I hadn't even realised I was carrying. I'd half expected to see Dad with his head on the crossbar, waiting for the blade to fall, waiting for me to be here to witness it. I'd half expected a scene of total horror. Instead, there was an eerie silence.

Kincaid had said to come to the Maiden, and here I was. But where was he?

Maybe he thought it'd take me longer to get here. Maybe we could actually catch him unawares ...

'The passage that led here from the graveyard ...' I turned, pointing in the general direction of Greyfriars. 'It was underground. Maybe we need to go down.'

'There's a basement,' Sebastian said. He tore his gaze away from the Maiden. 'It's where they keep the exhibits that aren't on display. C'mon, I'll show you.'

He led the way, past a clock and a canoe and an enormous lighthouse lamp, to a short flight of stairs down to the main entrance of the museum, in a vaulted Victorian cellar lined with works of art and signs to the different galleries. The main doors were glass, and they spilled weak daylight into the room. I hung back from them, aware that any passer-by could look in and see us. We couldn't rescue Dad or the twins if we got ourselves arrested.

Sebastian headed straight for the door marked 'Staff Only', and we stepped out of the sleek and beautiful museum and into a poky space with plain white walls and a flight of stairs heading down. The door swung shut behind us, and we were plunged into pitch darkness. I reached for the light switch, but Seb batted my hand away.

'If we're trying to sneak up on him ...'

'Crap. You're right.' I pulled out my phone and turned on the torch.

At the bottom of the stairs, there was another door, and I pushed it open. The room beyond was also black, but something about the feel of the air told me it was bigger – much bigger. I held the door for a second, listening, hearing ... nothing. Then I flashed my torch around. It glinted off a pair of staring white eyes, and I twitched back, before realising I'd seen eyes like that before, and recently.

'This is as bad as Isobel's house,' I muttered, stepping

forward and shining my torch down on a stuffed wildcat, which had been posed for eternity in a hunting crouch, butt in the air and teeth bared. It was sitting on a cabinet with a few other animals – and pieces of animals. Tiny rodent skulls gleamed in a neat row beneath a glass case, and a pair of bat wings, without the bat, hung suspended from near-invisible wires.

As I shone my torch beyond the cabinet of animal remains, I saw that the room spread out into what looked like a huge office space – a labyrinth of cubicles and cabinets, except that as well as papers and printers, the desks held strange treasures and pieces of art.

I hesitated, listening carefully, my heart starting to thud against my chest. I did not like this. I couldn't see anything beyond the small circle of light cast by my phone.

'I think there's a door right ahead,' Sebastian whispered.

I shone my torch ahead, but it didn't reach that far.

Right. OK.

I clung on to the naginata, holding it in front of me with the torch beam glinting from it and dancing on the ceiling and the relics on the desks, which I tried not to look at too closely – far too many of them seemed to have blank and staring eyes, or cringing faces, or too many legs.

There was a click. Then running footsteps. I flashed the torch beam up, and Alex came pounding out of the dark, arms pumping, blue eyes fixed on me. I yelped and brought the naginata up between us, twisting it around, thinking to smack him across the face with the blunt end. He skidded to a halt and I missed him by millimetres and struck a clay pot that fell from its desk with a valuable-sounding *crunch*.

'Run!' I turned and shoved Seb back towards the door and he didn't need telling twice. I put my head down and charged for the stairs, taking them as fast as I could in the dark with my torch's beam swinging erratically.

We burst out into the bright entrance hall and Sebastian immediately tripped and sprawled on the marble floor. I heard his teeth smack together as his chin hit the floor. I scrambled over his legs, nearly falling down with him, but then righted myself and bent down to help him up.

I managed to get one arm around Sebastian and help him halfway up the stairs to the gallery, before I felt the pressure on my neck. Clinging to the bannister with one hand, Sebastian and my blade both in the other, I could do nothing but freeze.

'Stop running,' said Alex, his voice dispassionate, his breath hot on my ear. I squirmed, hating the memory of how much I had wanted him.

He twisted my arm back, and I tried to clench my hand around the naginata, but it dropped from my fingers and clattered to the ground. Without me to hold him up, Sebastian lost his balance and fell back down the stairs, gasping and flailing. Alex had me in a solid armlock and I could only watch in horror as Sebastian rolled over, his head striking the marble step, and landed in an unmoving heap at the foot of the stairs.

CHAPTER NINETEEN

'Submit, and the Witch Pricker will make your death swift,' Alex said, without an ounce of feeling, as if my death meant no more to him than a grocery list.

'Never,' I snarled. I planted my feet against the step and pushed back, hoping I could throw myself backwards on to the steps and crush him under me. But he barely shifted. I twisted and writhed and looked down towards his feet, thinking I could bear him to the floor with a kick to the back of the knee, but he shifted his grip on me and lifted me right off my feet.

I threw an elbow back at his face, and felt it connect, but Alex barely flinched.

'Where's my father?' I yelled, throwing another elbow, feeling it connect, but still being carried up the steps. 'What have you done with the twins?'

'He will kill them soon,' Alex said.

We got to the top and he threw me down. I sprawled, tried to get up, but his hand twisted in my hair, sending sparks of pain down my scalp, and I screamed and clawed at him as he dragged me towards the Maiden.

But through the pain, and the volcano-hot fury, one thought persisted in my mind: they were *alive*. He could've lied. It would have hurt me to know that I was too late. He had no reason to say they were alive if they weren't.

I clung to that thought and muttered a breathy, 'Screw you!', as he lifted me bodily and slammed me against the black wooden upright of the Maiden. My breath blew out of my lungs in one strangled cough. I bunched my fists and pummelled them into his ribs, punching through the pain, until I felt something crack, and I saw sparks and black ink swirling around the corners of my vision.

But it was no use. I sagged back, gasping a panicked, painful breath of air. He wasn't keeping any sort of guard – he clearly couldn't even feel the punches that'd cost me so much.

And now Alex's hand rose to my throat, and he forced my head down towards the cutting bar.

Then, he stopped. He didn't relax his grip, but it became … stiff. I looked around, expecting to see Kincaid coming in to gloat. But he wasn't here. Alex had just … stopped.

'Millie,' he said.

Tears of shock and rage sprang to my eyes. '*What*? Are you threatening my *dog* now?'

He didn't reply. He wasn't even looking at me, his eyes were unfocused, gazing over my head. I tried to throw off his grip, and landed another punch on the side of his neck so hard that it immediately flushed red and began to bruise. He didn't flinch.

'Millie is short for Millions,' he said, through gritted teeth. I could see the muscles in his jaw jumping and twitching, as if he was trying to say something more.

Then he sagged. His grip dropped from my neck and he staggered back, hunching over his broken ribs, letting out a wail that reverberated around the empty gallery. He looked up at me, tears in his eyes. 'Diana,' he gasped.

But if he was going to say anything more, I never knew what it was. He straightened as if drawn up on invisible strings. As if his rib wasn't broken, as if he didn't even remember what had just happened. The tears spilled down his cheeks, but his face had turned back into stone, and he didn't waste time wiping them away as he reached for my throat again.

I was ready for him this time, and I ducked away and under the Maiden's crossbar and ran. I made it to the stairs and saw the naginata and Sebastian's unconscious body below me, and then I heard the screeching *skree skree skree* and I looked over my shoulder.

The moths poured down right on top of me and I screamed and I slapped at the chittering squeaking things that'd landed on my shoulders, in my hair, across the back of my neck and my arms. The moths settled, folding their wings together until they looked like hands gripping my arms, packing in more and more until they *felt* like fingers digging into my muscles. Their bodies shifted and merged, turned darker, turned into greasy, scratchy black fabric. I smelled decayed flesh and foulness.

'Have you come to accept your fate, little one?' Kincaid drawled.

I writhed, determined to throw him off, but he clamped his other hand over my forehead and let fly with another energy wave that blinded me and left me twitching and limp, unable to fight back, as I was dragged back once more towards the guillotine. I hit the platform face first and struggled to push myself up.

173

I was vaguely aware of Alex standing by, passively watching, and then Kincaid bunched his fists and thrust them towards Alex, who fell twitching to the ground.

'Must I remake you again, boy?' he sneered. 'When I'm done with these witches, we will begin. Understood?'

Remake?

Again?

'What did you do to him, you greasy prick?' I gasped, still trying to get up, though the world spun and swayed around my head.

A gobbet of nasty pinkish-yellow spit landed right by my hand and I flinched away.

'Disgusting,' Kincaid said, without irony. 'Such foul things come from your mouth. I shouldn't be surprised. You come from a long line of nasty little girls.'

'Why me?' I stumbled to my feet. 'What's so nasty about me?'

'You are an *abomination*,' Kincaid said, real anger in his voice. 'All your foremothers are abominations. I had your foremother's head on my block, but her sisters in corruption tricked me into losing her.'

I tried to get the Maiden between us, but he moved too fast and my reflexes were sluggish. He grabbed my head before I could stop him, digging his broken, yellow fingernails into my cheek, twisting and forcing it down towards the cutting bar.

All I could do was grip the wooden frame of the Maiden and brace myself to push back. I thought of all the people this terrible, terribly simple object had killed, and how many had done nothing to deserve it.

Foul smoke, and the sounds of women screaming.

My power. I could feel it, in my mind. I could feel exactly what it was doing, exactly where it lived within me. For the first time, I *understood* it.

I just had time to think, *Yes, and that's going to be so very useful if he chops off my head.*

But then I was lost to the sensations, dragged down under a rising tide of horror.

It was dark, and cold.

Icy flagstones burned against my wounds.

A man snarled in my face and thrust a long iron pin into my flesh, again and again, and his snarls turned to laughter.

I screamed with fury and struggled against my captor's hands as vial after vial tumbled from their shelves and smashed on the floor of my workshop, years of study and work shattering and dribbling away.

And then . . .

I was standing on a slick wooden platform, rain battering my face, and I was myself.

I gasped at the cold and the wet. It was so dark, I could barely make out the Maiden in front of me, its blade gleaming in the flickering torchlight. I looked out, over the crowd in their thick cloaks and bonnets, over the cobbled street that stretched away up the hill, and saw the silhouette of the castle looming down on me, more firelight dancing dimly on its battlements.

People were on the platform with me. Men in red coats, shouting. I looked around, confused and disorientated. Nobody here could see me, I was certain – I was like a ghost to them.

There was a woman on her knees by the Maiden. She looked up, hair hanging in matted ropes over her face, and I felt a jolt of recognition. This had to be Elspeth. There, arguing with the soldiers, was Kincaid – he looked completely different, so alive, and yet exactly the same.

I saw it all happen, saw a young Isobel storm the platform along with her Demon Hunter comrade. I saw Kincaid grab Elspeth, saw her raise her hand, her purple mark glowing.

And I saw her mouth something, something I couldn't quite

175

make out. She looked so sad, so tired. I knew her heart was about to give out, and she would die here, knowing that they hadn't even killed Kincaid.

But more than that. I felt connected to her, as if I could almost hear the words she was trying to say, and feel her desperation to say them. I hurried over to her, stood in front of her and tried to read her cracked lips.

'What is it?' I whispered. 'I'm here. Tell me.'

'The ... ba—' But her words stuttered to a halt, her eyes rolled back in her head, and she began to slip away ...

It was Kincaid's foul, rotting-flesh smell that dragged me back to my senses. I blinked, stunned that I still *could* blink, and took a deep breath.

Kincaid was grunting. One of his hands was raised and tugging at the peg from the Maiden, the one that would release the rope that would send the thick iron blade crashing down on to my neck.

It was stuck.

A voice shivered through me. *Kincaid. He lives.*

Another. *No, it cannot be.*

He has the girl.

I raised my head, my jaw going slack. I could feel something cold moving near me, around me, *through* me.

He has nothing, see, she hears us.

Then let her be ready to run ...

I felt tears prick my eyes. They had come back with me: the spirits of the women who'd been sacrificed on the Maiden, killed by John Kincaid and by the demon that squatted in his skull. Each one killed for the heinous crime of simply existing. I could feel them in my head, looking out through my eyes, urging me on, holding me tight.

Their strength was born of loss, and their fury ran so deep that it felt like calm.

176

I threw my head back and my skull connected hard with Kincaid's nose. Before he could recover, I spun on the spot and grabbed him into an outer hook throw that would have made Sensei Dave proud, wrapping my arms around his neck and shoulder.

Maybe Demon Hunters in his day were more into boxing and swordplay, or maybe it'd just been a while since any girl had got close enough to throw him, but the look of astonishment on his face as he flipped and went down was priceless.

In class, we were taught how to safely pin an opponent so they would have to tap out, or aim a swift and careful debilitating strike to an attacker. But screw that. I kicked him hard in the ribs and felt something snap. I aimed my next strike at his face, and the next at his solar plexus, hoping to wind him. I kicked him again and again and again, dancing back each time, light on my toes, so that he couldn't reach out and grab my ankle.

It was deeply satisfying. And he didn't get up ... yet. But, as I beat him, I could feel the spirits fading away. My pauses for breath grew longer, and Kincaid refused to lose consciousness. He was muttering under his breath, foul names I didn't think people from the seventeenth century even knew. I felt another one of his ribs snap and, in the next strike, I split the skin across his nose, but he didn't even bleed.

How do you kill a dead man?

He chuckled horribly. 'What's wrong?' he gurgled. 'Are you starting to wonder what will happen when you tire?'

I snatched enough breath to kick out at him again, but this time he rolled his shoulder and my foot glanced off and I fought for balance.

'Let me tell you, you silly little witch,' he snarled, his voice

177

thick and muffled, but steady. 'I will knock you down and you will suffer what you've given me *tenfold*. And when you're too broken to do anything but lie down and bleed, I will fetch the boy, and I will make you watch as I take his head.'

I swallowed, feeling icy cold. *Sebastian*. I couldn't see him from here, he was still lying at the bottom of the steps – he could have concussion, he could be *dead*. Guilt rolled over me like fog, clouding my vision for a second.

'Weak men deserve no mercy,' Kincaid muttered. 'I think I'll kill you *last*. I'll lay you at the foot of the Maiden and make you bathe in the blood of your family. You've brought them to me one by one.'

I let him ramble, my exhaustion catching up with me, my head spinning.

He was right. He would kill them all.

I couldn't stay here. Couldn't get to Dad. Couldn't get to the twins. Not without him killing Sebastian.

Kincaid was starting to get to his feet. I made my decision. I let out a desperate '*Hai!*' and twisted around into a roundhouse kick that struck him square in the face.

His skin splintered and shivered and disintegrated into a mass of chittering black and brown insects. His whole body crumpled and then rose again as the moths spiralled up in front of me, shrieking.

I turned and ran, channelling every last bit of my remaining energy into speed, every breath spurring me on. I took the stairs four at a time and landed heavily beside Sebastian – still out cold, could be dead, I didn't have time to check. I heaved him on to my shoulder in a fireman's lift and snatched up the naginata. Getting back to my feet was agony, but just as I thought I might not make it, there was an angry buzzing behind me and the fear spike pulled me upright.

I twirled the naginata in my hand so that the lacquered

wooden handle was pointing forwards, and then struck it against the plate glass of the museum's main doors. It shattered into a thousand dull safety-glass chunks, hanging suspended, bound together by plastic covering, and I hit it again and again, until the plastic tore from the frame and the whole pane crumbled to the floor.

I felt the telltale prickle of the moths trying to alight in my hair, but then I was through the door, Sebastian's thin limbs swinging as I sprinted out into the bright morning sunshine.

I would be back. For Dad, and for the twins. Somehow, I would save them.

CHAPTER TWENTY

I'd been behind he wheel a couple of times while ghost-hunting with Dad – a few laps of a private estate with the eccentric owner who had directly contradicted all of Dad's driving advice and just barely saved me from crashing into a wall.

I let out a stifled shriek as I fumbled for Ruby's gearstick and twisted her steering wheel as hard as I could, terrified I wasn't going to make it around the next corner. We skidded slightly on the turn, but we made it.

I didn't know this town. I didn't know where I was. I didn't know what I'd do if I was pulled over while driving *super illegally*. I didn't know if Sebastian was going to be all right. I didn't know how I would save my dad, or Minerva and Vesta. I didn't know if I was far enough from the museum to stop Kincaid coming after us, or if I was about to crash and finish his work for him. All I knew was that I couldn't stop.

I passed something I thought might've been a stop sign,

but I couldn't spare a thought for the rules of the road right now, not when I was focusing every last brain cell on just keeping the car going and not hitting anything or anyone.

I gripped the steering wheel and whimpered as a T-junction loomed in front of me. 'OK,' I gasped. 'Keep it together Diana, you can do this, just drive.'

I picked a direction at random and shot off down a steep cobbled street. Bad choice. It was so uneven that Ruby *bounced* down it, her 1970s suspension not really cut out for this kind of thing, and I hit the brakes a little too hard in my desperation to slow down. They gave a protesting screech and I was thrown forward against the wheel. There was a thump as Sebastian rolled off the back seat where I'd dumped him and into the footwell. Ruby rolled on, at a slightly more reasonable speed, but still shaking like a waterbed in an earthquake.

A moment later, I heard a groan, and a pale and shaky hand grabbed on to the back of the passenger seat.

'Di? What's happening?'

'I . . . I . . .' I shook my head. 'I don't know! Don't ask me questions right now!'

'Diana, can you *drive*?'

'I'm giving it a whirl,' I said through gritted teeth.

'OK, *stop*!' He put his hands on my shoulders and squeezed. 'It's OK, you can stop. Just ease down on the brake. Gently! It's all right, you can just stop in the middle of the street, there's nobody behind us. I promise. Just stop.'

My hands were almost shaking too hard to do anything at all, but finally Ruby rolled to a stuttering halt.

'We have to get away from here,' I gasped, my breath still coming fast and hysterical.

'We're all right,' Sebastian said again, soothingly. 'I don't think anyone's coming after us. Why don't you let me drive?'

'You can't, you might have concussion!'

But Sebastian was getting out of the car and opening the driver's door, pushing gently but firmly so I'd scoot across to the passenger seat. He rubbed his eyes as he sat down and belted in. 'Better an actual licensed driver with possible concussion than a hysterical beginner.'

'All right, but be careful!'

'Ruby won't let me down,' he said. He put her in gear and eased us forward at a swift but comfortable speed. 'You're such a good girl,' he added, and I blinked at him in surprise before I realised he was talking to the car. 'You looked after Diana for me, didn't you? You're so good, I'm going to get you a whole new gearbox when we get out of this.'

We drove in silence for a few minutes, before Sebastian turned to me and said, 'So, where to?'

Suddenly I wasn't actively problem-solving my way through not being able to drive. Suddenly, I had time to look at what I'd done and really *experience* the panic.

'I don't know ...' My voice wavered and Sebastian threw me an anxious look.

'I'm going to pull us up here, OK?'

I sniffed and wiped away tears. Sebastian said nothing more, and I was grateful for it.

I ran away. I just ran. Kincaid's going to kill the twins, he's going to kill my dad ...

I stared out of the window, but I wasn't seeing anything that was really there. All I could see was Dad's head on the Maiden, Dad's windpipe crushed under Alexander's fingers, Dad hanging from the ceiling like one of the museum exhibits. Every death I imagined I tried to squash, but the images were like weeds, new ones sprouting up as fast as I could pull away from them.

I ran. I left him there to die.

Sebastian pulled Ruby up into a narrow street and parked her deftly in between a white van and a giant yellow skip. He leaned on the wheel and blew out a long breath through his teeth.

'What happened back there? I fell ...'

I tried to tell him about Alex, and Kincaid, and the ghosts. It came out in broken shards of sentences, punctuated by hesitations and bitter silences as I tried to get myself under control and not lose myself to panic. 'And you didn't see what he did to Alex,' I breathed. 'What he said. I think Alex is under his control, except he tried to communicate with me, he repeated something I said on the train about my dog.'

Sebastian was giving me a deeply sceptical look, and I sighed.

'I know it sounds a bit nuts, but it was like he wanted me to know that he'd heard me, that there was a part of him that *cared* about my dog. And then just for a minute he could feel pain.'

'So Kincaid's henchman is brainwashed.' Sebastian shrugged. 'So what?'

So, I may not be a total moron for trusting him, for a start, I thought, but didn't feel like saying. 'So, he's a victim too,' I said. 'He may not be the person I thought he was, but there is a person *in there*, I'm sure of it. I have to help him if I can.'

Sebastian rubbed the back of his head gingerly. 'But how? How can we save your dad and Vesta and Minerva, let alone Alex too?'

'I don't know.' I swallowed painfully over the lump in my throat. 'Maybe Isobel was right. We weren't ready. *I* wasn't.'

Sebastian twisted in his seat to face me and chewed one knuckle, just a bit, and then said, 'What happened in the graveyard? Tell me again. How come you couldn't get him in your magic net thing?'

'We . . . we did.' I sniffed. 'We had him. It was working. He started *melting* . . . but then . . .'

He'd just stood there gloating – well, melting and gloating. What had he said? *I cannot be destroyed. My bond to this body is too strong.*

'It wasn't working, I mean, not like Isobel said it would. He said he was too strong, he couldn't be destroyed.'

I frowned at Sebastian, and he frowned right back.

'That's not right,' Sebastian said. 'I've read all the Demon Hunter reports, centuries of them, they all say that once the host is trapped there's nothing the demon can do about it.'

'He could've been bluffing,' I muttered.

'Maybe. Or maybe there's something else about Kincaid we don't know. Something Isobel hasn't told us,' Sebastian said darkly.

I sagged back against the passenger window. 'Doesn't narrow it down. I don't know if you know this,' I added, with a slightly crazy, brittle grin, 'but I've been a Demon Hunter for about thirty-six hours. She didn't even tell me that Mom ran off and abandoned you all.'

Sebastian ran the edge of his knitted tank top through his fingers nervously. 'I . . . I'm sorry about all that.'

'Don't be. You didn't know me, and anyway, that's what happened. She ran away to California, to live a life without any demons in it. I get why, now. I don't know how it doesn't screw you all up, growing up knowing you're descended from this line of goddamn *heroes*, people like Elspeth who *died* . . .'

I sat bolt upright, my rain-frizzed hair brushing the low ceiling of the car.

'*Elspeth.*'

Sebastian cocked his head. 'What about her?'

'She was trying to say something. I saw it, in my vision. She said the . . . beh . . . something beginning with "b". But she

184

couldn't get the words out.' I realised my knee was jiggling of its own accord, electric hope and nervousness coursing through me. 'Maybe there is something about Kincaid we don't know, but she did.' Elspeth ... the whore, Kincaid had called her, and anger flared red hot under my cheeks.

With the last few beats of her heart, she had been trying to help her friends to destroy the man who'd killed her.

'I mean, that's great,' Sebastian pointed out gingerly, as if speaking to an overexcited toddler. 'But if she never got the words out, I mean ... she's four hundred years *dead*. How can we find out what she was going to say?'

I knew.

I wetted my lips, not quite able to believe I was about to suggest this. 'The head. Elspeth's head. Kincaid left it in that room. I can go back ...'

'And do what?'

'... use her head to See.'

'With a *corpse*?' Sebastian said, so loud I actually shifted in my seat and glanced around in case anyone had been passing the car and heard him.

'Do you have a better idea? Or *any* other idea? I'm really, really open to suggestions.'

Sebastian looked horrified. But he didn't speak.

'For Dad,' I said, mostly to myself, swivelling back to face front and fastening my seat belt. 'For Vesta and Minerva.'

For them, I will do this thing. This awful, horrifying thing.

'Let's go.'

185

CHAPTER TWENTY-ONE

I made Sebastian drop me around the corner from the entrance to Greyfriars Kirkyard and promise to drive back to Isobel's as soon as I was out of his sight.

'Someone has to tell her what's going on. And, look at it this way,' I said, 'if I succeed, we can get a cab home and, if I fail, we won't need a lift. Ever again.'

'I wish you wouldn't say things like that,' Sebastian said. 'You're as bad as Vesta.'

'I'm going to take that as a compliment.' I thought about shaking his hand, or giving him a hug, but decided it was too cruel. Better to fake confidence. I gave him a bright smile, fished the weapons bag out of the back seat, and climbed out of the car.

'Diana! Wait.' He leaned over to peer up at me. 'I really am sorry about before. You're new to all this, but here you are – well, I'm never, ever going to doubt you again.'

'If I succeed,' I reminded him.

'Either way,' he said, and I shivered a little, but smiled. 'Good luck,' he called.

I waved, turned around, and didn't look back when I heard Ruby's engine kick into gear and her battered tyres roll off down the street.

I didn't know what Isobel would say when Sebastian got to her, but I was pretty sure she would be unable to help.

It was all up to me, now.

It was drizzling, the grey clouds settling back over the city like a comfortable blanket. The streets were busy for a Sunday morning, and I was intensely glad that I'd emptied out Sebastian's bag of weapons and stashed the naginata back inside so I could carry it without being immediately arrested. Frankly, it still looked a bit sketchy, but it was the best I could do.

I rounded the corner and hesitated, staring up the slope towards Greyfriars and the museum.

There was a large crowd gathered around the museum entrance, too large for the pavement to hold, muttering and milling anxiously. Stressed-looking police officers were patrolling around the edges. I hugged the side of the building and just watched for a moment, my heart in my mouth. What would happen if they tried to storm the building? It hadn't occurred to me to just *call the police*. So why were they here?

Most of the police I could see were trying to get the crowd to move on, or at least stop them getting run over by the passing traffic. I thought someone must have spotted the broken glass at the museum entrance by now, but that would hardly attract a crowd like this ...

And then my brain caught up with what I was seeing, and I groaned. There was a distinctly nerdy, gothy, fanatical kind of vibe among the crowd. I had my theory confirmed when two boys hurried past me towards the crowd, clutching copies of *Outrageous Occult Occurrences – an Obsessive's Guide*.

I lurked in the shadow of the Greyfriars gate, fished out

187

my phone and, feeling utterly ridiculous, opened Twitter and started searching the hashtags. It didn't take me long to find what I was looking for.

They were calling it #NMShaunting or #NMShostage – NMS for National Museum of Scotland. Rumours were flying thick and fast, but a few things everyone seemed to agree on:

1. Jake Helsing had been last seen going into the museum, and hadn't tweeted anything for nearly twenty-four hours, which was a red flag to his fans, who had come to the museum to investigate.
2. A fan had spotted the broken glass doors and reported them to the police.
3. Police had gone inside, and hadn't come out again. The museum was now surrounded and on lockdown.

I clutched my phone so tight in my shaking hands that I was afraid I might break the case.

If the police were in there with Kincaid, they were probably dead. How long before the SWAT teams descended, barged in and were slaughtered – or spooked Kincaid into killing Dad, and the twins, whether he had me too or not?

The only thing worse would be if the amateur ghost-hunters got in *first*.

I had to find Elspeth's secret, before this turned into a bloodbath.

The gate to the Covenanters' Prison had been chained up, at some time in the last hour or so. I swore under my breath as I turned the heavy padlock in my hands.

There was nothing else for it: I heaved the naginata over the top of the gate, looked around just in case there was a phalanx of Scottish policemen behind me, and then clambered over after it.

I squeezed down the gap behind the mausoleum, pushing myself to go faster, to ignore the prickling of fear from being squashed into the thin space. After all, there was much worse waiting for me down below.

My heart gave a horrible lurch as I shone my torch down on the floor of bones and saw that some of them were smeared with dark red and brown. These were the tracks I'd left, ancient blood sticking to the soles of my shoes as I'd fled Kincaid's trophy room.

The chamber beyond the doorway was completely dark. The candles must have burned down. *Great. Alone in a room full of severed heads, in the dark.*

I didn't dare check the battery on my phone. I knew it would be running down, and fast.

Find Elspeth.

I forced myself to raise the beam of my torch, running it over the floor, familiarising myself with the dust and the spatters of ancient clotted blood, until I found the first head, and then another. Then I flashed the light around the walls and up on to the ceiling, because I was damned if I was going to fall for a tired horror movie trope like getting snatched from above.

There was nothing waiting in the shadows to leap out at me. Not that I could see, anyway.

'All right,' I said, as loud as I could force myself to. 'Let's have you, Great-great-grandma. You and me need to have a talk.'

I tried to breathe evenly, as I propped my phone in one of the empty candle sconces so that its light bounced back from the stones all around. Then I knelt down, settled back on my heels, and reached out with shaking hands to take the head that rested in the catacomb marked *Elspeth, the Whore*.

Elspeth still had a thin head of stringy, dark hair. Her skin was cracked and desiccated, but her flesh still had some give in it.

I laid my palm gingerly on her forehead, like a faith healer who'd arrived much, much too late.

Nothing happened, and I withdrew my hand with a shudder.

No. I can *do this*, I thought stubbornly. *I've done it before. This ... This is real.* I shouldn't have been able to surprise myself with a thought out of my own head, but somehow the idea had crept up on me and I blinked down at my hand.

This is all real. None of this is imaginary. None of this is a game. I'm really a Demon Hunter, my dad and my new sisters are really hostages, I'm really kneeling in the muck, in a graveyard, with my hand on the head of a dead woman, and she is really going to speak to me.

I forced myself to sit up and reach for Elspeth's head in one motion, because if I didn't I was afraid I wouldn't be able to. For a second nothing happened, and then it came to me:

A wall of cold air. I gasped and reeled. White snow swirled in front of my eyes. The sky above me and the ground under my feet were both completely white, and the only clue we were still in the city was a dark stone wall to my left which was not quite completely covered by the snow.

A baby's scream destroyed the peace of the moment. Out of the whirls of snow, a dark figure loomed. He knelt down, black cloak spread behind him, and a patch of dark stone in front of him where the snow had been brushed aside. On the stone, a writhing shape screamed and wailed helplessly.

I walked closer, my skin crawling.

He had cut the baby across the back of one arm. Blood dripped on to the frozen stone.

'Answer my call, Oriax.' The young Kincaid's voice wavered. 'Come to me!'

The swirl of snow abruptly changed direction, and on the whistling wind I heard a voice answer him: Why do you call me, servant of death?

The voice was like ... like glaciers moving, and steel traps snapping shut, and nothing like either of those things. Oriax ... was that the name of the demon who was still riding around inside Kincaid's body?

'I need your help,' Kincaid said, through gritted teeth. 'I need to rid the world of them. The witches! All the wicked women who smile and defy God and do not know their place. I've prayed to God to help me, but He does not answer!'

What will you give me? The disembodied voice was thick with hunger. If I help you do this?

'The life of my own son,' he said. 'And my body, so that you can walk in the world after I've gone.'

Then we have a deal, said the ice-and-grinding-metal voice of Oriax.

Kincaid raised his knife and, even though I knew I couldn't change the past, I started forward, desperate to stop him hurting the baby any more.

But before I could get to him, a dark-haired figure in a grey cloak skidded around a corner. She held a wooden quarterstaff in her hand and brought it around to smack Kincaid across the chin, sending him flying back and the knife spinning away into a snowdrift.

It was Elspeth. Tears had frozen on her cheeks and her eyes were red and angry. She scooped up the child and stepped back, holding Kincaid away with the end of her staff.

'You will die for this,' she yelled, and then wrapped up the child in her cloak and turned and ran.

I felt a presence at my side, and looked up to see ... Elspeth,

191

standing beside me. She looked much older, and she turned and met my gaze steadily.

'You must be the Seer,' she said. 'My descendant, daughter of Kara, daughter of ... oh, so many others.' She turned to look at where her younger self had vanished into the snow, but there was nothing there.

'What happened to the baby?' I asked her.

'We sent him far away. Kincaid never found him.'

A deep sigh of relief hitched in my chest, the cold air burning in my throat.

But it wasn't over. Kincaid was getting up, spitting blood on to the snow.

So, *said the echoing whisper on the wind again, and Kincaid threw up his hands to shield his face as the snow whirled faster around him.* The child has been taken. What, now, will you give me?

'Anything!' Kincaid shouted, and opened his arms. 'Take me now, use me as you will – only promise me that you will kill that witch!'

It is done, *said the voice, and the snow rushed into Kincaid, through his open mouth, his ears, his nostrils, even into his eyes. Kincaid screamed.*

Darkness folded over me.

'He invited the demon in,' Elspeth's voice whispered in my ear. 'He gave Oriax his consent. It cannot be torn from him. John Kincaid himself must renounce the demon in his mind.'

My eyes blinked open and I found myself back on the floor of the tomb. After the snow, the stone felt almost warm.

Elspeth's head had rolled out of my hands and lay nearby. I set it gently against the wall, and then hauled myself to my feet, vibrating with fury.

He was going to kill that baby – not just any baby, but his own *son*.

He made a deal with a demon, invited it into his heart, and for what? Revenge on Elspeth, on 'witches', on any women who didn't fit into his narrow, stupid idea of how they should behave.

I tore away the crumbling paper label from Elspeth's catacomb, and shredded it into tiny little pieces.

'I'm going to get him,' I told her. I took my phone from the sconce on the wall and started to ascend, back up the passage towards the light.

CHAPTER TWENTY-TWO

I squeezed out of the space between the mausoleums and shook myself out.

'I told you!' a voice hissed, and I jumped and snatched up the naginata.

'Um ... Hi!' said another voice. I blinked towards the padlocked gate to the rest of Greyfriars Kirkyard, and felt my heart sink. There were four or five kids over there, all about fourteen years old, and all staring right at me. 'Diana Helsing, right? Jake's daughter? It *is* you?'

Oh boy. *Helsingites*.

I hesitated, wondering if I could plausibly deny it. Not really. I was trapped in the Covenanters' Prison, and it wasn't as if there was anywhere to run, except back down into the hidden tomb. I sidled towards the gate, hoping I wouldn't be visible to any stray priests or police who happened to walk past. I held up my hand to my lips, trying to shush them.

'How did you get in there?' said a girl. 'Is Jake here? Is he all right?'

'I told you,' the boy who'd spoken first said again, impatiently, 'I saw her come into the graveyard and then climb over the gate.'

I frowned at the two of them. The girl seemed familiar. She was tall, with red hair, and cute ghosts on her scarf.

'Hey, it's you! From the book launch!'

'You recognised me,' the girl said, blushing bright red. 'Wow. So, what's going on?'

'Nothing,' I said quickly. 'Nothing's going on.' I realised as soon as I'd said it that with dust and blood in my hair and all over my nice new jeans and jacket, holding something suspiciously weapony in one hand, red-eyed and smelling of dead things, and with Dad already missing, I probably wasn't all that convincing.

'Come on, please,' said another girl, who was really rocking the scary-raccoon look when it came to eyeliner. 'The police won't tell us anything. They say we're making things up and now they won't even send more people in to search, but we know he's been in the museum all night, and someone or some*thing* smashed the front door out, and now here you are, creeping into locked graveyards.'

'Listen,' I said to the Helsingites, as a potentially genius brainwave struck me. 'I need to get into the museum. Dad's in there. He needs my help. Something occult *is* going down in there, something absolutely genuine and really serious. I have to get in, but we have to keep all civilians out, and that includes the police. Can you guys help me?'

'I knew it,' the boy whispered.

'I dunno how you're going to get in,' said the raccoon girl. 'There are like fifty police on the entrance now.'

'What about the back door? Down the alley, behind the fence?'

Their blank looks were all I needed. This could work.

'Here.' I put the naginata back into the bag and squeezed it through the bars of the gate. The red-headed girl took it gingerly. 'Is anyone looking?'

The Helsingites looked around, and then shook their heads. I hoisted myself up and over the gate, and dropped down clumsily on the other side.

'All right. All I need is to get through the crowd to that alley without the police or any of the fans stopping me.'

One of the boys, a broad-chested kid with a temporary bat tattoo on his neck, unzipped his hoodie and held it out to me. 'You'll blend in better.'

'Thanks,' I said, and shrugged it on over my jacket, pulling the hood up and making sure that most of my hair was safely tucked away inside.

'We'll carry the – this – between two of us,' the tall girl said, holding out one of the straps on the long black bag to the boy. He took it gingerly. 'If we keep it at knee height it'll be less obvious.'

My heart swelled two sizes as I looked into their thoughtful, eager faces, and I swore I would never take Dad's fans for granted again.

'So is this going to be in the new book?' bat-boy asked, as we made our way at a hyper-casual saunter out of the Greyfriars gate and up the road towards the museum.

'I think this might be a little too *real* to go in a book,' I answered honestly, and rather than seeming disappointed his face broke into a broad grin.

'*Awesome.*'

The Helsingites formed a human shield all around me as we reached the crowd, quietly elbowing and excusing their way past the little clusters of people. 'Over there, see it?' I muttered to the redhead. She nodded without looking at me.

'Police on our six,' said raccoon-girl quietly. 'Keep going, don't look.'

'On our six?' one of the boys muttered. 'Where'd you get that from?'

'*Call of Duty*,' said the girl. 'We're almost there, just keep walking.'

A towering man in the biggest leather jacket I'd ever seen shuffled politely out of the way for us, but a group of women dripping with silver pentagrams were more of an obstacle and we had to sneak around them. They were chewing at their black-painted nails, staring up at the building.

Finally, we came to the end of the alley. I could see the fence, and knew that the wooden door was just on the other side, still unlocked. All I had to do was—

'Hey, you lot, come away from there!' said a very adult, very unamused voice.

'Oh crap,' I groaned.

'Don't look, just go,' said the redhead. She handed me the bag as subtly as she could, which was not very subtly at all. 'We'll keep them busy.'

I hesitated for a minute, then whispered, 'Thank you, guys!' and took off at a low run, clinging to the wall of the alley.

'Hey,' the policeman said again, and then I heard the sound of five fourteen-year-olds making as much noise as they could all at once. It was a lot of noise.

'Excuse me! Sir! Hey! We need help! Our friend's hurt! Someone took my wallet! Hey, you can't go that way! I need help!'

I didn't stop running. I couldn't look back. I gripped the naginata inside the bag and used it like a vaulting pole, boosting myself up on to the gate. I scrambled for a foothold and nearly fell back, but managed to throw myself over.

There was shouting, but I didn't stay to find out what it

was. I burst through the door and into the marble corridor, shutting it behind me. I looked around, just in case Kincaid was camping at the door waiting to grab me, but there was nobody there. I seized one of the heavy stone benches, bunched my muscles and dragged it across the floor with a horrible scratching noise, setting it down so that it blocked the door.

The sounds of shouting faded and died.

I peeled off the boy's hoodie, and then unpacked the naginata. The blade gleamed. I tried to feel reassured.

So here I was. Back in the wolf's den, all alone.

Shake it off, I told myself. *Find the twins. Find Dad. Then you won't be alone any more.*

I came out into the bright white gallery, and shivered as I saw that it was lit up with blue flashing lights, streaming in through the windows. I could hear the static roar of the crowd and an announcement through a loudhailer that was completely unintelligible.

There was no sign of the police who'd come in earlier.

I really, really wasn't keen on walking past the Maiden again. Instead, I skirted the edge of the gallery and headed up a stopped escalator to the second floor.

Standing at the balcony looking down on the Maiden and the lighthouse lamp and the distinct absence of demons or Demon Hunters, I felt even more keenly the enormousness of this place. But all I could do was search, and keep on searching until I found them. Or they found me.

I had three doors to choose from. The first I picked was labelled 'Romans and the Divine', and I could see it was a dead end, but I crept to the far end anyway, just in case the twins were tied up somewhere, gagged or unconscious. But there was nobody there, except for the marble heads of Emperors, gods and monsters.

I looked up, and my eyes met a pair of painted eyes that gazed out from a golden frame. It was Diana, the Huntress – probably modelled after a real person, because she was actually wearing clothes. She wore a golden circlet with the crescent moon on her forehead, and was holding a bow and raising her hand to shade her eyes.

She was searching for something, too.

I reached up and touched the necklace that Isobel had given me, the open palm smooth under my fingertips. If there was any real charm in it, I hoped with all my heart that it would help me now.

I only wished I could follow their tracks, like the Huntress, chasing down the stag with her hounds at her heels . . .

Wait a minute. I gave the painting one more glance, and then hurried out of the gallery and back to the corridor. I had a choice: I could turn left or right, or I could go on up the stairs to the next level. My heart in my mouth, I knelt down and pressed my hand to the floor, like a real hunter listening for the vibrations in the earth that marked the passing of their prey.

I heard footsteps, and voices. My head flew up and I looked around, half expecting Kincaid to come stomping up the stairs, but the footsteps drew closer, and closer, and there was nobody. *It's working*, I realised, and felt a thrill shiver down my spine. I was Seeing with the *floor*. Amazing. I closed my eyes to listen more clearly.

The footsteps came closer, and closer, until they were right on top of me.

'*Take them,*' *Kincaid's thick, slurred voice growled.* '*Keep them quiet. Let her come to me before you kill them.*'

There was a muffled cry of anger, low and frightened. It had to be Dad.

The footsteps started again. Dad's muttered curses started to move away ... up the stairs in front of me. Other, heavier footsteps were moving to my right. Alex? There was another noise with him. It was the sound of something being dragged across the floor.

I opened my eyes. A knot of tension in my temple was threatening to turn into a thumping headache, but I knew what I had to do. I had to choose who to follow – upstairs to Dad and Kincaid, or right, following the trail of Alex and the twins.

It was an easy choice, as long as I thought like a Demon Hunter. I glanced up towards the next floor and my hand strayed over my heart.

I will find you, Dad. When I have the power to free you, and not before. I need my sisters first.

I stood up, rolled my shoulders, and turned to the right.

My heart was beating so loud, as I wove my way through the galleries, I thought it might give me away. At each new room, an extra shot of nervous energy surged through my veins, until I was clutching the naginata to my chest as a way to keep my hands under control.

I took readings from some of the objects on display. A collection of Maori art gave me nothing but the taste of salt water and warm air, but when I ran my hand over the surface of an ancient pair of bagpipes, I could hear, above the faint wailing notes, the sounds of something dragged along the floor, high and slurred Scottish voices, and then a loud and musical crash. I looked around, and saw – yes, a South Asian instrument of some kind had been knocked over. They came this way. I had to keep moving.

More galleries, more silence. I ran my hand along the ribcage of a wolf skeleton that had been posed in the act of leaping on its prey, and felt it snarling in my ear. But the thing that stopped my heart for a moment was Vesta's voice – trembling, terrified. 'Please, don't hurt her!'

I gripped the naginata more tightly, and stepped slowly towards the next doorway – then stopped, forcing myself not to gasp out loud.

Four police officers were lying slumped against the wall. For a second I feared the worst, but there was no blood. I hurried to them, my own breath stalling in my throat, and held my trembling fingers to their pulses until I was sure: all four of their hearts were still beating. They were alive, but simply out cold.

Letting out a shaking sigh of relief, I stepped into the next room.

It was darker than the others – one wall of the room opened on to the balcony and grey daylight, but the others were painted black and dotted with stars and galaxies. The glass cases in the middle of the room held chunks of glittering rock, crystals and geodes and those ones that look like tiny models of glowing cities.

I hesitated in the doorway, and that's when I heard the breathing sounds, loud and raw and definitely not coming from the police in the next room. I pressed my hands together, just to be sure. I wasn't touching anything but myself, but I still could hear it. Something shuffled, and then there was Vesta's voice again, whispering.

'Don't, it was an accident, just ... don't.'

They were here.

CHAPTER TWENTY-THREE

At the back of the room, behind a cabinet of gleaming crystals, Alex was holding Minerva with a long and jagged shard of glass pressed to her throat. The front of her neck was a red, sticky mess. I stifled a yelp of fear and grief, but then I realised that she was bleeding not from a slit throat, but from a scattered collection of tiny cuts.

From my hiding place behind a huge and glittering amethyst rock face, I counted at least twenty. Twenty times, he had cut her.

She stood there, frozen, with her head back, her chest rising and falling slowly. Vesta sat on the floor in front of them, her hands tied, and her eyes fixed on her sister. She was completely still, too, except for the occasional blink.

Alex didn't even blink. His face was back to that blank, impassive stare. He had two large bruises on his face and neck from where I'd hit him before, but he showed no sign of pain. I could barely tell if he was even breathing.

I was afraid for Minerva, afraid for Vesta and myself and

Dad, but I couldn't forget what I'd seen downstairs, not the desperate tears in his eyes when he'd said my name, and not the twitching when Kincaid had hit him with a blast of energy.

Did he already 'remake' you?

How long have you been under his control like this?

How long has he been hurting you?

My guts twisted at the thought, but I tried to shove the feeling aside. My sisters, my father, they were my priority. If the puppet Alex stood in my way then the real Alex was just going to have to deal with the consequences.

Just looking at him, standing with the shard held at Minerva's neck, made the muscles in my back and arms want to cramp up. It was a deeply unnatural stillness, and I was willing to bet that if Vesta moved, or tore out of the ropes around her wrists, or if Minerva so much as thought about producing a bolt of lightning, his reflexes would bury the glass shard in her throat before she could even scream.

It was very effective. So effective, it was working on me too. I didn't dare move in case I startled him into killing her.

What am I going to do?

There was no way I had a good enough aim to throw the naginata and not hit Minerva. The twins' weapons were on the ground by Alex's feet, so they were right out.

My only option dawned on me slowly and horribly, like the morning of a physics exam, when you've been cramming all night and you're still pretty sure you don't know any physics.

In order to not startle him, I was going to have to announce my presence – deliberately, and *carefully*.

I retreated into the previous gallery, minding my footsteps, and then very deliberately walked back, letting my feet fall heavily. No surprises.

I heard a gasp, and thought, *That's it, I've killed her*, and then Alex's voice – impassive and firm – saying, 'Be quiet, or she dies.'

I forced myself to walk out into the space gallery and stand where Alex could see me.

I met Minerva's eyes, and hers widened. Her lips trembled, as if she was desperate to speak, but simply didn't dare. Vesta was seated with her hands tied and facing away from me, but I saw her shoulders sag just a little.

'I'm here,' I said.

Alex looked from Minerva to Vesta to me.

'I will kill her,' he said, and jabbed Minerva's throat again with the end of the glass shard. She whimpered, and I shuddered, and gripped the naginata tighter than ever, so hard I could feel the wrapped strings around the handle digging in and leaving stripes across my palms.

'Then you will have disobeyed him,' I pointed out quickly. 'He said not to kill them until he has me. Right? Well, here I am, still free. If you kill her before me, you will have disobeyed his orders. He doesn't like that, does he?'

Just for a moment, the mask slipped. Alex's eyes widened, terror painting his skin bone-white. The hand holding the shard of glass dropped away from Minerva's neck and trembled, hard.

Minerva screamed out a few short syllables of Gaelic and threw her hands up. Short, stabbing bursts of energy crackled from her fingertips. Alex yelled and staggered back, the glass falling from his grip.

Vesta tore the rope from her hands in a shower of hemp threads and clambered to her feet.

'We've got you now, you big wee bastard,' she snarled.

Alex recovered, his blank expression back in place, and threw himself at Minerva. Minerva danced out of the way and Vesta tackled him to the floor.

'This'll teach you,' she said, laying a punch on his shoulder that made something audibly crunch. 'To leave my sister alone!'

But something inhuman was driving Alex now, and he barely made a sound before he threw her off. She crashed backwards into one of the cabinets and shielded her face as more glass shattered and rained down on her.

'V, down!' Minerva shouted, and lobbed another bright lance of light at Alex's head, but he rolled aside and it struck a towering chunk of speckled rock, leaving a scorched scar across its surface.

I leaped between the exhibits and brought the naginata down in front of him as he lunged for Minerva one more time. He skidded to a halt just short of running right into the blade. I spun it around and caught him a smart whack on the side of the head with the handle end.

His eyes followed the blade as it whirled back towards him, like a cat watching a fly. Behind him, I could see Vesta reaching the twins' weapons, grabbing her sickle and Minerva's crossbow and bolts. She threw the bow to her sister and brought her sickle around, ready to dig its wicked curve into Alex's neck.

Alex didn't look around, but he ducked, so Vesta's arm swept harmlessly through the air and her sickle scythed across a display of glittering blue and purple quartz, sending the heavy rocks crashing to the floor. He twisted to land a punch on her chin and she staggered back, colliding with the huge amethyst crystal. It toppled slowly and hit the floor with a bang that shook the gallery.

A crossbow bolt crackling with white lightning whizzed over Alex's head and shattered the glass of another display case.

'*Shit*,' I heard Minerva hiss.

205

'Di, get in position!' Vesta yelled, as Alex turned back to me. I tried, but couldn't find the spot.

'Everything's in the way,' I yelled back, 'I can't—'

Alex scooped up one of the huge, heavy purple quartz lumps and raised it to throw. I was a sitting duck, trapped between two glass cases. I raised the naginata and cringed back, hoping to deflect the rock as it came at my face, but then Alex lobbed the quartz low. It struck my leg and sent me crashing to the floor, howling as the pain burned and blossomed over my knee.

I couldn't get the staff up in time to block him as he came down on me, fist first.

Silly demon. The floor is where I do my best work.

I caught his driving fist, using the energy in it to twist him around and bring him down on his back with a thump. Sitting on his legs, I gripped his shoulder, and squeezed on the place Vesta had punched him. He didn't register the pain at first, but then his eyes rolled back in his head, and he gasped and let out a high-pitched groan. His arms went limp and I pinned his wrist, and my other hand closed around the glittering lump of quartz. I hefted it in my hand.

Then he looked up at me, and his chest hitched with pain and terror. His expression turned soft, his blue eyes met mine. His lips were trembling.

'Alex,' I said, my arm lowering just a bit. 'Is that you?'

'No . . .' He could hardly get the words out, but he looked around and his gaze fell on Minerva, stalking towards him, her crossbow raised and her throat a bloody mess from the cuts he'd made. He looked back at me, and he raised his chin, resolved despite the pain. 'Do it,' he said, through gritted teeth. 'Can't . . . trust . . . *do it!*'

I gripped the quartz and brought it around and slammed it into his temple.

He went limp and his eyes fluttered closed.

I dropped the quartz and sat back, shuddering.

'Jesus, Diana,' Vesta said. She put her arms around me and lifted me off him, setting me on my feet but not letting me go. I gasped, pain throbbing through my leg and tears streaking my face, but I could stand – my knee felt weak, but I didn't think it was broken.

'Is he out?' Minerva asked, stepping gingerly over Alex's prone legs. 'Are you OK?'

'*Me?*' I gasped, wiping away the tears and staring at the bloodstained front of Minerva's top.

'I'm fine,' she said, although her hand shook as she raised it gingerly to her throat. 'They're only small.'

Vesta bent down and handed me the naginata, and I leaned on it, while she ran over to her sister. She hugged her gently and peered at her cuts. 'I'm so sorry, Min, I tried to stay still.'

'Don't be an idiot,' Minerva said. 'Just … find me something to wrap around it.'

The three of us limped and shuffled out of the devastated space exhibition towards the light. I leaned on the white iron bannister, catching my breath, stretching my leg this way and that, testing the strength of my knee. The Maiden still squatted in the middle of the gallery like a black insect, and the orange and blue flashing lights were still casting anti-shadows across the white marble floor down below.

Vesta ran into the next exhibition, and came back a minute later with a scarf woven in geometric patterns of black and orange.

'Hey, woah.' Minerva held up her hand. 'I'm not bleeding on someone's sacred ancestral … tablecloth, or whatever.'

Vesta and I both stared at her. I don't know about V, but my heart felt like it was growing about twelve sizes.

'It's brand new, ya wee nerd,' Vesta said, a strained laugh in her voice. 'It's modern art.'

'Oh, well in that case.' Minerva took the scarf and wrapped it carefully around her throat.

'Suits you,' I said.

Minerva smiled. Then, as one, we came in for a hug, holding each other gingerly, careful of our wounds.

'Are you two all right?' I asked. 'It took me so long to get to you, I'm so sorry.'

'We're fine,' the twins chorused.

'What about your dad?' Minerva said, pulling away, her hands on my shoulders.

'Kincaid has him.' I shuddered, and looked up. 'Somewhere up there. You guys, the things I've seen in the last hour ... the women, the torture ...' I glanced back at Alex, who was still out cold, sprawled in a starscape of broken glass.

'You know, we made a *lot* of noise just then,' Minerva pointed out.

'Yeah. That's OK, he knows I'm coming anyway. This is a trap.' I glanced at the others, and couldn't help a smile crawling across my face. 'He wants to get me and he's used my dad as bait. That was his mistake.'

'Di,' Minerva said slowly, 'are you all right? You look a bit ...'

'Crazy,' said Vesta.

Suddenly our moment of peace was disrupted by a wailing noise that splintered the air around us. I gripped the bannister and looked up, before I realised it wasn't the sound of a person in pain. It was the sound of another police van drawing up outside, its sirens blaring. I guessed that here, finally, came the SWAT team.

'Let's go,' said Vesta, grabbing my hand. I paused, looking down at the unconscious Alex.

'Should we leave him here?' Minerva wondered aloud.

'If we kill Kincaid, maybe he'll be free from the spell, or whatever it is,' I said hopefully.

'Maybe,' said Minerva, not sounding too convinced. 'Let's just hope, if he wakes up, it's Jekyll and not Hyde who comes after us.'

We retraced my steps through the galleries to the stairs. The twins' footfalls were heavy, and their breathing laboured. My brain ached, and I really wanted not to invite any more people into my head, but I had to check, so I put my hand down on the bannister and concentrated.

As soon as I heard the echo of Dad's muffled shouts I tore my hand away.

'Yep. That way,' I said, cradling it to my chest.

Minerva put a steadying hand on my back. 'Wow, that's amazing!'

'Let's go,' said Vesta. 'C'mon, Seer. We've got you.'

I steeled myself and started to climb.

'I found out why the net didn't work before,' I said. 'Kincaid invited the demon in. He gave it permission to possess him, and that's why their bond is stronger than ...' I paused, suddenly out of breath. The pain in my knee was flaring, and I leaned heavily on the naginata.

'So what do we do?' Vesta asked, looking from me to Minerva.

'Catch him again. Get him in the net. Then, we have to get him to renounce the demon, Oriax.'

'How?' Minerva panted behind me.

'I'm not sure,' I admitted, 'but I'm thinking lots and lots of pain might do the trick.'

The next level up was the top floor of the white iron gallery. The glass roof was right above us, and the rooms seemed to be laid out just the same as the floor below. I did not like the idea of fumbling my way around the galleries again. But then the twins spread out to search, and after a moment Minerva waved for my attention and beckoned us over silently. She had found a small, winding stone staircase. A cold breeze hit me as I looked inside. The door at the top must have been opened.

They were on the roof.

Vesta led the way, her sickle held ready to strike. I followed, levering myself up each step with the naginata, my knee twinging and threatening to give out. Minerva brought up the rear. I could hear the click-clack as she loaded her crossbow. The stairs were thick, plain grey concrete and they spiralled higher and higher, until finally we stepped out of the stairwell and saw Kincaid.

His cloak blew around him in the wind so he was a wavering dark shape out on the roof. Against the bright cloudy sky and the pale brick and metal, he looked like a bad stain on clean, grey cloth.

'Welcome!' Kincaid crowed.

CHAPTER TWENTY-FOUR

I felt my stomach turn over as we stepped slowly across the flat roof towards him.

Dad was standing on the end of a wooden sleeper, like from a railway line or the beam of an old building, hanging over the edge of the roof like a pirate about to walk the plank. Except with less hope of survival, once he dropped. The weight of the wood was balanced so that it wasn't tipping – not yet. But all Kincaid would have to do was push, just a little, and it would topple over. That was if Dad didn't manage to fall off all by himself first – he was wobbling, his hair flying in the stiff breeze. He was gagged, and his hands were tied in front of him, so he couldn't even reach out to steady himself.

His eyes were uncovered though, and he saw me step out on to the roof. His eyes widened. He shook his head. I tried to meet his gaze steadily, to reassure him somehow that I was going to save him.

'I love you, Dad,' I called out. 'It's going to be OK!'

I saw tears spill over his cheeks and whip away into the empty air below his feet.

Minerva and Vesta were moving away from me with each step, trying to flank Kincaid so that we could get him into our net of power. My heart hammered, and panic started to grip me once again, my attention split between the girls, Dad and Kincaid.

How do you make someone renounce a demon they've lived with for hundreds of years? Is there even a real John Kincaid in there any more?

The police sirens were much louder up here, and now there was another sound being borne up towards us on the wind – the sound of people screaming.

The Helsingites had seen Dad. Could they tell from down there that it was their hero balanced on that beam, about to fall? Either way, they were freaking out.

'That's close enough,' Kincaid snapped, and all three of us stopped at once. 'One little push, and your father will be splattered across his adoring fans. The mortal police are on their way, but they won't be here in time to stop me.'

I heard a clanging sound from behind us. Footsteps. I looked around, half hoping it was the police, half dreading what Kincaid would do ...

But it was Alex who emerged from the stairwell.

He looked like death. His cheeks and eyes were sunken and dark, and I swallowed back a shudder. I felt as if I could see right through his skin to the bones of his skull.

'Alexander,' said Kincaid. 'You have allowed these girls to defeat you twice. You have failed me. You will pay for that, when we are done here. Stand by the father, while I destroy these worthless worms.'

Alex didn't flinch, and my heart sank. He stood to attention and gave an emotionless little nod, and then skirted stiffly

212

around me and Vesta to stand by Dad's sleeper. I twitched as I saw him place a foot on the end of the wooden plank. One kick, and it would all be over.

Kincaid smiled at me, hideous yellow lips twisting. 'Or perhaps I'll order him to do it now. Let you watch as the man who gave you life is destroyed by the boy who has your heart.'

The who? I frowned, completely thrown. My eyes met Alex's and I flushed, horrified and embarrassed all at once.

'What are you talking about? We went on one date. *Half* a date, and then he tried to kill me! You archaic, sexist, *raging asshole*,' I said.

'Watch your language when you speak to me,' Kincaid snarled.

I actually felt a laugh bubbling up in my chest at the sheer absurdity of him. 'You know, everything you think about the world is wrong. Pretty much every single thing. Anyway, thanks to you I've never met the real Alex, have I? He was under your thrall the entire time.'

Kincaid stepped towards me, treading carefully to avoid being caught between the three of us. 'If you try to flank me, Minerva, Alexander will throw her father from his perch,' he said. 'If you think that she will ever forgive you for causing her father's death, go right ahead.'

Minerva glared at him, but stayed still.

'As for the "real Alexander",' Kincaid said, moving closer and closer to me, 'ask yourself this, girl: why would I bother constructing a fake personality for such a worthless object? I have been inside the boy's head. I've seen his true heart.' Kincaid shook his head, a disgusted snarl splitting the skin across his mouth. 'Shallow, stupid boys, letting their lust trick them into trusting witches like you. Into wanting to *help* them. I have seen his heart. It is ... compromised. He will be useless to me, when you are dead. I expect I will order him to jump.'

I shuddered, feeling compromised myself, and glanced at Alex again, but his face was a mask of perfect indifference.

He's just saying all this to throw you off, it's probably all lies. Don't fall for it. Focus!

The words of Master Yeun from Vesta's ju-jitsu class suddenly flashed into my head. *Be so strong that nothing can disturb the peace in your mind.*

I had to block Kincaid's manipulating, lying words out. I had to focus on destroying him.

Kincaid reached into his robe, and he pulled out a long, metal needle with a handle made from pocked bone.

'I'm going to bleed you,' he murmured. 'Just like I bled your foremother. I will drive this into you until there isn't an inch of your skin I haven't pricked. You will beg for death. You will confess your sins. Then, and only then, will I let you die, alone and afraid, in the dark, like you have died in your dreams a thousand times before.'

His words were horrifying. But I let them wash over me, his posturing and his threats, and they started to feel ... desperate. *No new information here*, I thought. *Evil misogynist is sexist and evil. Film at 11.* And finally, I tuned him out altogether.

'Please, don't,' I said. 'Don't hurt—'

And then without warning I spun, shifting my grip on the naginata so it swept out in a wide circle. It sliced through the air and caught Kincaid hard on the side of the face, blade edge first.

Kincaid reeled, and a new split tore across the skin on the side of his face, but there was no blood.

Minerva and Vesta both moved, seizing the opportunity while he was distracted. I braced myself for the rush of power, but it didn't come. Kincaid rushed me with a furious roar, the needle glinting as he raised it up over his head. I swung the sword round again and dodged back, trying to keep him at arm's reach. Over his shoulder, I saw Vesta skid to a halt and back up.

Every move I made, they had to compensate – but if I stayed still, I would be dead.

Minerva raised her crossbow and fired a crackling bolt right towards us. This time, her aim was true, and it struck Kincaid in the back. He howled, and dropped the needle. I swung the naginata like a golf club and sent the needle spinning off across the roof, out of Kincaid's reach.

'I got this, get in position,' I yelled, planting my feet on the roof, determined not to move an inch. I swung furiously at Kincaid, but then he ducked under the naginata and grabbed on to the handle. A wave of slicing energy ran up its surface and leaped into my arms. The world went white and I crumpled against the hurt, and the next thing I knew, the naginata was out of my hands and I was on my knees on the cold brick of the roof.

'Pathetic children,' Kincaid snarled. He threw the naginata to Alex, who caught it easily. 'Kill him!'

My heart felt like it was twisting itself inside out. Vesta and Minerva both turned to sprint for the edge of the roof, but they weren't going to make it.

'No!' I leaped up and shouldered Kincaid aside, running towards Dad, but my knees were still weak and he easily bore me back down to the floor, one hand on my chest, the other clutching in my hair. The impact winded me and Kincaid held me down, helpless and gasping while Alex raised the sword, swinging it around towards Dad.

No, no, not now …

But Alex had hold of the blade end, and now the handle was extended towards Dad.

'Grab it!' Alex shouted.

Dad must have been as stunned as the rest of us, because he actually hesitated.

'Come on!' Alex yelled again, his voice cracking, his other hand going to his side to cradle his ribs. 'I don't know how long I have!'

I thought my heart was going to explode with relief. Alex's chest heaved with the pain he had been pretending not to feel. Dad wrapped his bound hands around the handle and Alex pulled him in, extending a shaking hand to grab the lapel of his jacket. Dad stumbled forwards, and for a sick second I thought he might fall. The crowd below shrieked, and then roared with joy as Alex got an arm around Dad's shoulders and helped him back on to the roof.

'No!' It was Kincaid's turn to shriek in anger. 'How did this happen? I made you and remade you, how did you regain control?' He reached out a hand and I saw the air flow around it. I used all the breath I had to throw my elbow back into Kincaid's ribs. He gave a satisfying *oof* and the rippling air vanished.

'Alex, get him out of here!' I gasped. Our eyes met. Alex hesitated for a split second, gazing at me, still trapped under Kincaid's grip. Then he nodded and grabbed Dad's arm.

'No, Diana, I can't, not without you,' Dad shouted, but, even injured and shaking, Alex was the stronger of the two and he dragged Dad bodily towards the stairs. As he did he tossed the naginata to Vesta, who slid it fast across the roof towards me. I snatched it, and felt a rush of relief at the sensation of my hand back on its smooth lacquered surface.

Kincaid's hands came down on my neck. I didn't have room to swing the sword, and flashing spots of light crossed my vision, then a crackling blaze of fire hit Kincaid square in the shoulder and he flew off me, smoke billowing from his cloak.

I heard Vesta's laugh, and running feet. Kincaid was on his back. This was my chance. I rolled on to my knees, brought up the naginata and plunged it down in the middle of his chest.

He looked up at me and laughed. He wriggled, like an insect pinned to a board – except less human. A slow ooze of black blood trickled from his mouth.

'You didn't really think your weapon could kill me, did you? I can't die, you fool!'

But killing him wasn't the plan.

I steeled myself, and before he could let off another wave of pain I planted my palms firmly on his disgusting face, and threw myself headlong into his mind.

CHAPTER TWENTY-FIVE

Snow swirled all around me, but it felt more like sand, or shards of glass. I winced and threw my hands up to shade my eyes – thin cuts opened up all over my face and hands, and closed again as quickly as they came. My head felt like I was getting a frontal lobe lobotomy without anaesthetic, and I couldn't see a thing.

But I pressed on, because I was damned all the way to hell if I was going to go through this and not find John Kincaid.

'I know you're in here!' I screamed into the whiteness, feeling the shards cutting across my lips and melting on my tongue. 'Face me, you coward! Stop hiding behind your demon and face me!'

I recoiled as another flurry hit me and a wave of pure, stomach-churning hatred passed through me. I had a short, nasty flash of what it must be like to hate everything, all the time. Was this the inside of Kincaid's head, or Oriax's? Was there really any difference any more?

I stumbled forwards, forcing myself to focus all my thinking on the things I loved in this world. My dad. My mom. Millie. The twins. Edinburgh, London, Maisie – oh God, what the hell was I going to tell Maisie about all this?

And, suddenly, I was out of the blizzard and standing on thick, soft snow. It was like being at the eye of a tornado – the whirling shards formed a white wall around me.

Something dark was huddled in the middle of the calm space. It was John Kincaid. He looked up as I approached him, and I saw that he was young again, his hair long and brown, his skin clear, but he looked skeletally thin, as if he'd been starved. Or maybe as if the demon had eaten him up slowly from the inside. He saw me and recoiled.

'You're her,' Kincaid spat. 'Stay away, witch! Stay away! Oriax, protect me . . . You should be wiped off this earth. You and all your kind. You corrupt men, corrupt their souls.'

His words washed over me, harmless except that I knew they were driving something much stronger than he was. He was weak, deep down in himself. He always had been.

'The corruption in your soul is you,' I said. Then I did something that seemed to terrify him even more – I smiled at him. 'Have you seen the world recently? Women fighting wars, curing diseases, ruling entire countries. Women everywhere, wearing trousers and doing jobs and . . . and going into space.'

'Shut up,' he muttered. 'Your words mean nothing to me.'

'Just stop fighting me,' I said. 'You don't have to be afraid any more.'

'I . . . I can't,' Kincaid slurred, self-pity crumpling his haggard features. 'I can't rest. I just want to rest.'

'I can give you death,' I said, and the way he looked at me, I knew that I had him. 'You should have died hundreds of years ago, a bitter old man. I can give you that now. Renounce Oriax, and you can go.'

John Kincaid stood up. His limbs were so thin I thought they might crack underneath him.

Come on, you can do it, *I thought.* Be brave, for once in your sorry, pathetic life.

'I – I renounce you!' he shouted into the swirling snow. *'I renounce you, Oriax!'*

There was a shriek, and the snow swirled blood red.

I woke up on my back, Kincaid standing over me, the naginata in his hands and a dark split in his chest where it had pinned him. His face twisted so hard in anger the splits in his skin were stretched and globs of black blood dribbled out.

'Curse you!' he screamed. 'Curse the disloyal, lying coward who gave me this body!' He raised the naginata to bring it down into my heart. Then something large and grey struck him and he flew backwards, dropping the sword. The grey thing clonked on to the ground beside him – it was a lump of concrete, trailing metal.

'Diana, what happened?' Vesta asked. As I scrambled to my feet I saw her turn back to the edge of the roof and rip another chunk of concrete right out of the parapet.

The crowd was shrieking again, and someone was screaming through a loudhailer, but I couldn't make out the words.

Vesta hefted the concrete as if it weighed no more than a football and then lobbed it at the head of the thing that used to be Kincaid. He dodged, this time, and the concrete smashed to pieces on the roof behind him.

'He's done it,' I gasped. 'He's broken the deal. That's not Kincaid any more.'

'Get in position!' Minerva called us, loading her crossbow once more.

I moved instinctively, my eyes on the figure as he balled his fists and summoned up another heat haze, but aware in some back-brain animal sense of exactly how far I was from the twins.

The sword cut was still oozing black blood, leaving a trail behind him as he stalked unsteadily over the roof towards me.

The demon let his energy wave fly towards me and I braced myself. It sliced through me and I stumbled but I didn't fall down. Minerva shot a crackling bolt of lightning towards him, and it struck him in the chest, right in the sword wound. A burst of red mist spattered from it and he reeled.

We were in formation now, flanking him on all three sides; we just had to find the exact spot.

'Freeze, both of you,' I yelled. 'I can do this!'

The twins stopped moving, and I stepped back, looking for the place.

The demon raised his hands and a pulse of energy hit me square in the chest. I staggered back and there was a scream of horror from below me as my foot struck the parapet.

I glanced down. Hundreds of tiny faces looked back up at me, pointing fingers, shouting. Blue lights on the police cars strobed over the crowd, dizzyingly far down.

I twisted back to face him and planted my feet in the steadiest stance I could, sure he was going to rush me. Minerva fired another crossbow bolt, but it struck his back and he didn't even flinch. He was still muttering curses and slurs under his breath, threatening me with ultimate, painful retribution. Vesta was on the floor, trying to dig her fingertips into the roof and prise up a hunk of concrete to throw.

I feinted right, and then stepped left.

The body's yellow eyes didn't leave mine. 'I will crush you against the ground below and paint the walls with your blood,' he said.

I fixed my eyes on him, tried to think of something smart to say.

'Nah,' I said, and stepped left one more time.

'No!' the demon shrieked, but then his cry was cut off as he started to choke.

My head cleared. My knee stopped throbbing. I breathed

in a long, deep breath of cool summer air and smiled as Kincaid's corpse recoiled, writhed and twisted. Up above us, the clouds roiled and thundered, and a bolt of lightning shot down and struck the point between us, crackling back and forth between our outstretched arms.

This time, I kept my eyes open, and I saw them. The colours. The light flashed back and forth and split and wove together, every colour of the rainbow and several new ones that I couldn't name or even describe.

I felt weightless, and looked down, and laughed as I saw the surface of the roof drifting gently away from my feet. Vesta and Minerva and I hung in the air, effortless, crackling with power.

Then the power struck Kincaid's body, and he just melted away – it was disgusting, but at least this time it was quick. His skin slid and flapped off him like a badly fitted suit, blood ran thick and red out of the bottom of his robe, his bones crumbled as they were exposed to the air. A moment later, there was nothing left but a pile of ancient black cloth and a red puddle.

My feet hit the roof and I staggered and caught myself. I took a few long steps away from the edge, towards Minerva, avoiding the trails of dark red where Kincaid had moved around the roof.

'We did it!' I crowed. 'We actually did it!'

And about time, too – I could hear the loudhailer again, and this time it was closer, and it echoed – the police were inside the museum.

'Diana, look out!' Minerva yelled, and she grabbed my sleeve, dragging me forwards just as a shrieking chittering went up behind me. I staggered towards her, buffeted by something, and turned back.

A black shape rose from Kincaid's corpse, a shape made

of moths and smoke, solidifying and growing – six feet tall, eight feet . . .

It had two legs, and four arms. Its head was a black skull, with three pairs of blank, white eyes. On its back, moth-like wings fluttered. A red mouth opened right in the middle of its chest and let out a sound like a thousand death's head moths on fire. Searching, tentacle-like antennae unfolded from the top of its head.

I staggered back, snatched up the naginata and held it wavering in the air, its length magnifying the shaking of my hands.

'Now all we have to do is kill it!' Vesta said. 'Before the police get here!' She hefted the sickle in one hand and another lump of concrete in the other.

I looked from the hideous, shrieking thing to Vesta and back again. 'Oh, good,' I said faintly, before the demon lashed out with one hand and caught me a hard blow on the shoulder that knocked me to the ground. Lightning flashed from Minerva's hands, and the demon turned on her, twitching and reeling from the pain but still moving, ready to tear her apart.

I clambered back to my feet and leaped, swinging the naginata blade around hook-side first. It caught the demon's shoulder and tore through its skin – except it didn't seem to *have* skin, or blood or bone. It was the same thick black texture inside as out. Oriax reeled and screamed in pain.

Good. You can be hurt. I'll cut you to ribbons before I let you hurt my friends.

The demon's wings flashed out and I ducked and rolled to avoid being caught as they swiped through the air above my head.

I pulled back the naginata, aiming to swing it into the back of the demon's knee, but then I heard the sound of footsteps pounding on the stairs – many, heavy footsteps in steel toecap boots.

'Police, we're coming up!' yelled an angry female voice. 'Put down the weapons and keep your hands in the air!'

There was a horrible noise from behind me. The demon was laughing. 'Your police won't stop me, little creatures!' Its voice was like hundreds of tiny voices all speaking at once. 'I will tear them apart. I will eat their hearts!'

The stomping and the shouting were growing closer. I thought back to the murdered women, and Dad, and Alex, and even John Kincaid himself, and I ran at the demon.

No more. I won't let you hurt any more innocent people. This is my fight, not theirs. So let's see what terminal velocity does to you.

I heard Vesta and Minerva shouting, and picked up speed, my boots pounding across the roof. Oriax reached out its four hands to grab me, and I put my back into it and shouldered the thing as hard as I could. It had me in its grip, but its six white eyes widened and the mouth opened and the thousand tiny voices shrieked in terror as we both hit the parapet.

The crowd roared horror in my ears and I dug my fingers into Oriax's flesh as we overbalanced. The world turned over, and where there should have been roof, there was a sickening *lack*.

My heart thumped in my ears, measuring out time in flashes:

Thud, my hair whipped around my face.

Thud, we dropped towards the pavement.

Thud, the crowd was pushing and surging away.

Thud ...

Oriax writhed and spat out one last curse in a language that made my skin feel red hot all over, and then it disintegrated in my hands. Moths swarmed out of its mouth, swirled around me chittering and beating me with their wings, and then fluttered out of my grip.

I dropped, flailing, a thin scream in my throat ...

And then something clamped around my ankle and I swung back against the wall of the museum, hitting it with a *thunk* that made my teeth rattle. I screamed in pain as my leg stretched and twisted with a *pop*, and my arms slapped against the brickwork, hard enough to graze.

But I wasn't dead. I wasn't splashed all over the pavement below.

I looked up. Minerva's hair hung down like a blonde curtain, swinging wildly as she looked down at me. Her hands were around my foot. Her face was going bright red with the effort, but she smiled at me.

'Think you're gonna ... get rid of us ... that easy?' she groaned.

I peered up and past her, to where Vesta was leaning over the edge of the roof holding her sister's ankle with a lot less effort. She grinned at me.

I gasped and looked out over the city, hanging upside down over my head like a crazy cave roof of glinting stalactites. I was just in time to see the last of Oriax's moths flutter away and vanish.

It escaped. My face flushed, partly from the blood rushing to my head, but partly with desperate, exhausted anger.

We were alive. Dad was saved. Kincaid was gone. But this wasn't over.

I hadn't wanted to die. But if I'd just been able to hold on, to keep it from flying apart in my hands ...

'All right, officers?' Vesta said, somewhere above my head. I looked up and saw more faces peering over the edge at me, faces of people in hard plastic visors and bulky black body armour. 'Um ... I mean ... help?'

CHAPTER TWENTY-SIX

The door to the cell opened, and I sprang up off the blue plastic bed. The policeman on the other side of the door gave me a weary smile and stepped back, gesturing for me to leave.

I didn't need telling twice. I wasn't sure what time it was, but however long I had spent in that tiny room, with its scratched white walls and plastic-coated pillow and toilet in one corner, it was too damn long.

'Come with me, please,' the policeman said, and waved me on down the Institutional-Blue-painted corridor.

I hardly dared to hope, but then he unlocked a door with a keycard, and then another, and then I was stepping out into the reception of St Leonard's Police Station.

They were all there: Vesta, Minerva, Sebastian, Dad. They turned to look at me, and Vesta whooped, and then Dad was running towards me, and he nearly tripped over a chair, but then he was scooping me up in a warm, tight, slightly shaky hug. I squeezed him back and tried not to weep openly. I was fine, until I realised his tears were soaking into my shoulder.

I lost it then, clinging on to him for dear life, crying until my throat burned and my chest ached, until the tears slowly turned into hiccups of laughter.

We practically had to be levered apart by the policeman to finish doing the paperwork.

'How the hell did you swing that?' I hissed to Sebastian as the four of us finally staggered out of the station.

'I just waited until the shift changed, and then had a word with their computer. You were in for Breaking and Entering, so I changed it to Trespass and recommended a fine and release to a responsible adult. None of the new officers on shift knew the difference. When we get back to Isobel's I'll delete you altogether. No record of you even being in the museum.'

'Well, except for the officers who arrested us, and the massive crowd of people who saw me leap off the roof,' I pointed out.

'Oh, they were mostly fans – they love a good cover-up,' Dad said. 'This'll make their year!'

I stopped in my tracks to grab hold of him and hug him again.

As we walked into the car park, something caught my eye. The shape of a person, tall and lean, wrinkled dark blue shirt and dirty black jeans. He was lurking between two cars, and my heart skipped a beat in fear, but then I realised he was hunched, his arms wrapped around his ribs.

It was Alex. *Really* Alex.

I thought about how well it would go over with the others if I pointed him out, and then I said, 'Actually, I need to visit the little criminals' room. I'll catch you up.'

Dad slowed his walk and gave me a look as if he wasn't sure he wanted to let me go to the bathroom all by myself, but then Vesta linked her arm in his and asked him something about ghost-hunting, and he let himself be gently pulled away.

I slipped between the cars and approached the spot where I'd seen him, half afraid he would be gone. But then there he was, leaning against a police van, a stunning blue and yellow and purple bruise spreading all across the side of his face where I had stunned him with the hunk of quartz.

He smiled at me. An electric shiver of relief ran down my spine. His expression was soft, *real* – he still looked like he might be in pain, though not the stunning agony that had broken through Kincaid's brainwashing.

Kincaid's . . . or Oriax's?

How do you know it's really over?

'I . . . I think I broke your ribs,' I said. 'I'm sorry. Although not really.' I stared at him, still finding it strangely hard to believe that this boy had kidnapped my dad, nearly killed him, nearly killed me. And just as hard to believe that I was standing here talking to him now, as if nothing had changed since that first time we'd met on the train from London.

'I get it.' Alex smiled, and then winced as the skin stretched across his swollen cheekbone.

'Are you . . . ' *Better? Not evil?* ' . . . going to be all right?' I asked.

Alex nodded. 'Ach, yes. I think so.'

I heard a car door, and the unmistakable rumbling of Ruby's engine warming up.

'That's my ride,' I said, and hesitated, my hands plunged into my jeans pockets. 'Do you think we'll see each other again?'

Alex smiled. 'I'd like that,' he said. 'I owe you . . . more than you want to know. It might be nice to actually . . . *meet* you. For real, this time.'

I smiled back, but inside I suddenly felt a pang of sadness.

That's right. Whoever I met on the train and went on that date with … that person doesn't truly exist, no matter what Kincaid said. I've never met the real Alex.

But perhaps I would, in time.

'Did you know, for some cultures the bear is a very powerful occult talisman?' said Dad.

I leaned back against the cushions of Isobel's couch and smiled up at the looming stuffed animal that towered over us. Frankly, after the last couple of days, Isobel's weird hobby seemed really tame. I reached up and stroked the bear's soft brown paw. He was very fluffy. The fact that he'd been posed with his teeth bared as if he might chomp down on our heads at any minute was barely creepy at all.

'Nope,' I said. 'I had no idea.'

Vesta and Minerva were either side of me on the couch, all three of us covered in a thick, soft blanket and clutching mugs of hot chocolate in our laps. Dad was sitting opposite, in a stiff-backed armchair, looking around at Isobel's taxidermy collection as if it was the most interesting thing he'd seen all day.

He must be fine, I thought, a warm glow settling in the pit of my stomach. *If he's dispensing occult trivia nobody asked for.*

I had been afraid that Isobel would turn us away from her house when we got back, that she couldn't forgive me for choosing Dad over my own safety, that we would have to fight it out on the doorstep. But then she had opened the door in floods of tears, her hair loose and tangled at the nape of her neck, and she'd thrown her arms around all three of us, and then Dad, and then us again. The twins had to take her inside and sit her down, as if she was really their elderly auntie who was having some kind of attack.

She had wept for an hour straight, except for the moments

where she broke off to tell us how proud she was, and how sorry.

I still wasn't sure I'd really forgiven her for suggesting I let Dad go, but we would probably be OK. After everything I'd seen, I could understand her terror of the Demon Hunter line ending, even if I couldn't understand the lengths she'd go to.

'This is all so incredible, Diana,' Dad said, for the hundredth time. 'Demon Hunters! Real demons and Demon Hunters. In my own family!' He took a sip of his coffee. 'I always knew that your mom was special, but I never had any idea about all this.'

I rolled my eyes. Leave it to my dad not to seem shocked by any of this.

Of course, I knew better. I remembered how hard he'd held on to me, how much his hands had shaken.

'And this is ... for life?' he said, for about the fifteenth time.

Vesta and Minerva nodded in perfect unison.

'Diana is incredibly brave,' said Isobel, coming back into the room with a thick, leather-bound book held in her arms. 'You should be very proud.'

Dad looked up at me, a brief flash of fear clouding his face, but then it passed and he grinned at Isobel. 'Well, of course. Have you met my daughter? She's pretty amazing, you know.'

'I want you to have this, Jake. To welcome you to the family. The full history of the Hunter Trinities of Edinburgh and Scotland. John Kincaid, the Maiden, all of it is in here.' She handed the book to Dad, who took it and opened it to a random page and immediately started to read.

'Nearly all of it,' I said quietly. 'Kincaid's deal isn't in there.'

'Well, we'll have to write up that part and add it in,' said Dad. 'I'll help you, sweetheart, don't worry.'

'Dad,' I muttered, watching him flipping through the pages of the book greedily. 'You know you can't publish any of this, right?'

Dad looked up, caught my expression, and closed the book carefully. He reached over and took my hand.

'Diana, I'm sorry I didn't believe you, that first day,' he said. 'I've been useless, and I'm so sorry.'

I smiled and squeezed his hand, then let go. 'I think I'm technically still due a grounding,' I pointed out.

'Weren't you being kidnapped at the time?' Dad said. 'I think we can let it go, just this once. You bet I'm going to be much jumpier about knowing where you are from now on, though.'

'Fair.' I nodded, feeling my heart sink. 'Oriax is still out there. We killed the host, but God knows what the demon's going to do now.'

'Alex, too,' said Vesta. She glanced at me, and I avoided her eyes, wondering if she'd seen him in the parking lot too. 'We don't know if the demon's influence will wear off, or come back with a vengeance. He could be real trouble. We can't assume he's good now just because we want him to be.'

I flushed, despite myself.

'Or because he's incredibly hot,' Vesta added, her voice needling me.

'I mean, *right*?' I said, unable to help myself. 'I swear, anyone would've fallen for it, it's not just me.'

'I wouldn't have,' said Minerva and Sebastian in unison. I stuck my tongue out at them.

'Oriax is vulnerable now that he's out of his shell,' Isobel said thoughtfully. 'He will be much less brazen about his attacks. We may be able to find the boy first.'

231

I shifted in my seat, not meeting anyone's eyes.

I found him, or he found me. And I let him go. It didn't occur to me not to ...

'Maybe the demon will take the hint and sod off back to hell,' Vesta said hopefully.

'Oh, you'll find him,' Isobel said darkly. 'Demons don't give up that easily.'

'Just let us dream, OK?' Vesta complained. 'Just for like a day. Maybe two.'

'Evil never sleeps, dear,' Isobel admonished.

'Actually, I think there's something you should see,' Dad said. 'I think I can help you – if that's all right.' He reached into his bag, and pulled out an iPad. He turned it around so we could see the screen, and I vaguely recognised the map as being one of Edinburgh. There was the castle, the park, Arthur's Seat ...

The map was covered in little green glowing dots of varying sizes.

'What're those?' I asked, because I knew he was waiting for somebody to ask.

'I've been gathering information,' he said, practically lighting up with pride. 'I wrote an app for it! I started plugging in data sources before we moved here. Each dot is somewhere that someone has reported supernatural activity. And look at this ... ' He peered over and jabbed his finger at one particular location, somewhere right in the middle of the map. The dot over it was so big I couldn't even see where exactly it was pointing to. 'This is the Edinburgh Vaults.'

Vesta coughed slightly, and Minerva rolled her eyes.

'No offence, Mr Helsing – that place is meant to be haunted, yeah, but it's just a tourist trap.'

'That's what I thought. But in the last twenty-four hours,

this place has lit up like a Christmas tree. *Something* is happening down there. I think ... ' He frowned and tapped the screen, then shook his head. 'It's a bit buggy still,' he murmured.

As the cab pulled up to take Dad and me home, Vesta and Minerva pulled me into another three-way hug. We didn't speak. We didn't have to. I just looked into their eyes, and knew – our work would never be done, but they would have my back, until the very end.

We climbed into the cab, and gave our home address. I watched Isobel's house recede and vanish, and felt a knot of anxiety twisting up in my chest.

'It's not over,' I muttered. 'It's still out there.'

Dad took my hand. 'Diana, you need sleep. I'll call Isobel as soon as we get back and check in. The fate of the world may rest on your shoulders, sweetheart, but you can't carry it if you never get any rest.'

'But what if ... ' I began.

'No what ifs. Listen to me. I'm your dad,' he said. 'I'm here for *you*. Now more than ever. And if I'm not doing a very good job of it, you have my permission to kick my ass.'

I nodded. He was right, I was tired – and dirty, and bruised, and not in any fit state to save the world. I would save the world again tomorrow. I leaned my head against his shoulder and began to drift off.

The cab pulled up outside our house, and I clambered out, half blind with tiredness. As Dad paid the driver, I heard him say 'Hello, again, by the way.'

I turned around and blinked at him. He saw me looking and gave me a friendly wave.

'You probably don't remember me,' he said. 'I picked you both up from the station when you first moved in.'

233

I remembered. It was only a couple of days ago. It seemed like years.

'I saw you two on the news – good to see you're all right,' the cab driver said. 'How are you finding Edinburgh so far?'

It's terrifying. Exhausting. Bloody. Beautiful.

I smiled at him.

'It's home,' I said.